SPARRING WITH
BEATNIK GHOSTS
IN THE CHINATOWN DUNGEON

Sat. August 23rd

@ LUPO

8 P.M. TO 1:30 A.M.

916 GRANT S.F.

FRESH POETRY & LIVE MUSIC

$3 w/flyer

Feature Performances & Open Mic
(sign up in person or via email: dyaryan@att.net)
Produced by FUTUREMAN PROPAGANDA

SPARRING WITH
BEATNIK GHOSTS
(BORN: 8.23.08)

Round II — **SPARRING WITH** — Round II
BEATNIK GHOSTS

@ THE BEAT MUSEUM
NORTH BEACH SAN FRANCISCO

Wednesday, **APRIL 22, 2009**
7 p.m.
540 Broadway
NORTH BEACH
www.kerouac.com

featuring
Jazz Poet
CHARLES CURTIS BLACKWELL
Performance Artist
STEVE ARNTSON
San Francisco Poets
Jennifer Barone • Craig Easley
Ana Elsner • Gail Mitchell

& SPECIAL GUESTS:
Mission Poet
Alfonso Texidor
The Poetic Sounds of
LUNATION with Clara Hsu & Bill Mercer
& music by
BLACK EARTH & THE LAUGHING CHILDE

Produced/Hosted by Bob Booker & Daniel Yaryan

SPARRING WITH
BEATNIK GHOSTS
in Downtown Santa Cruz

POETRY MUSIC ART — POETRY MUSIC ART

Wed. **FEBRUARY 24** 7 p.m.
FELIX KULPA GALLERY
107 Elm Street Between Streetlight Records & Cafe Pergolesi

FEATURING

"The Frisco Kid" **Jerry Kamstra**
Marc Kockinos * **Pablo Rosales**
Singer **Hanna Rifkin** * **Len Anderson**
Bea Garth * **Nicholas Pierotti**
& Performance Artist **Steve Arntson**

PLUS: OPEN MIC POETRY | PRIZE DRAWING | ONLY $3

ROUND SIX **SPARRING WITH** @ VIRACOCHA
BEATNIK GHOSTS
998 VALENCIA, SF

Produced by **BOOKER & YARYAN**

sparring...
ruth weiss
with jazz by: Doug O'Connor, Hal Davis & Steven Faivus

GUEST HOST: MARC KOCKINOS

SATURDAY APRIL 24TH 6 P.M.

Avotcja
Alfonso Texidor
Mark States
Jessica Loos

COPUS
with: Royal Kent, Wendy Loomis, Patrick Mahon & Omar

Clive Matson
Mamacoatl
NKETCHI
Charlie Getter
Bethany Rose

$6 DONATION AT DOOR

SPARRING WITH BEATNIK GHOSTS

Round III
@
BIRD & BECKETT
Books and Records

653 Chenery St
San Francisco
GLEN PARK

GUEST HOST
PHILLIP T. NAILS

Saturday
AUGUST 15
7 p.m.

PLUS: OPEN MIC

Produced by
BOOKER & YARYAN

FEATURES:
Neeli CHERKOVSKI

Joie COOK

Steve ARNTSON

Jonathan SIEGEL

The Peruvian Poetess CAMINCHA

FEATURES:
Jazz Poet Charles CURTIS BLACKWELL

Will DODGER

XANDRA

The BOOKER & The BISHOP

With Special Surprise Guests

ROUND IV — SPARRING WITH BEATNIK GHOSTS — ROUND IV

IN "THE LAND OF THE DEAD"

@
FAITHFUL FOOLS
STREET MINISTRY

234 HYDE ST.
(Near Eddy)
San Francisco's Tenderloin

Produced by
BOOKER & YARYAN

TUESDAY NOV. 3RD 7 PM

pOeTrY LIVE
w/cOLLage aRt
by Guest Host
rAMu aKi

MYSTERY ??? POETS

WWW.FAITHFULFOOLS.ORG

SPARRING with Beatnik Ghosts

ROUND 7

VENICE
681 VENICE BOULEVARD

@ **Beyond Baroque**

SPARRING:
ELLYN MAYBE & Her Band
IRIS BERRY
MICHAEL C. FORD
MIKE THE POET
RACHEL KANN
B.G. PETRAKOS GARY JUSTICE JIM BOLT
PLUS: MYSTERY POETS

FRIDAY JULY 23
7:30

GUEST HOST:
MANI SURI
PRODUCED BY: YARYAN

SPARRING WITH BEATNIK GHOSTS @ THE RED VICTORIAN

Spoken Word & Music
1665 Haight St. S.F.

David Meltzer
Diamond Dave
Julia Vinograd
Debra Grace Khattab
Bob Booker
Marc Wilson
J. Brandon Loberg

Music by:
Alan Sitar Brown

Special Guest:
Jane Ormerod

Hosted by:
Gail Mitchell

Produced by Yaryan
Co-sponsor: BookSmith

SPARRING WITH BEATNIK GHOSTS

presents

Poster: Melissa West

TRIPLE SPAR

3

A SPOKEN WORD TRIPLE KNOCKOUT!

ROUND 9:
SAN FRANCISCO
OCTOBER 14, 7PM
THE BEAT MUSEUM
540 BROADWAY (AT COLUMBUS)
GUEST HOST...GINGER MURRAY

ROUND 10:
BERKELEY
OCTOBER 15, 7PM
ART HOUSE GALLERY
2905 SHATTUCK (AT ASHBY)
GUEST HOST...MARK STATES

ROUND 11:
SANTA CRUZ
OCTOBER 16, 7PM
FELIX KULPA GALLERY
107 ELM STREET
GUEST HOST...MARC KOCKINOS

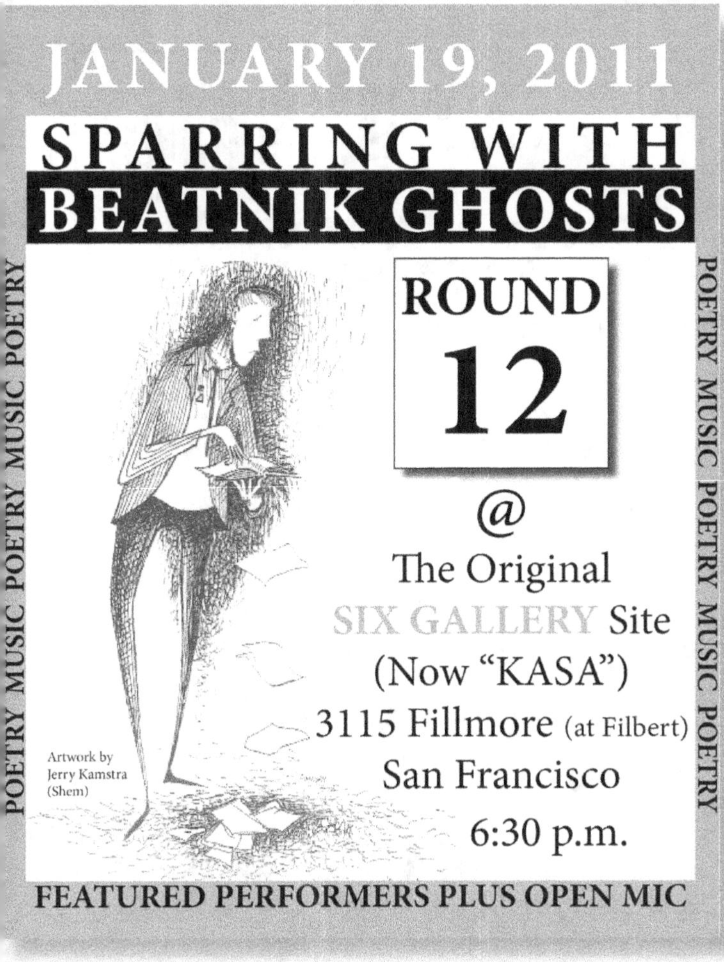

JANUARY 19, 2011

SPARRING WITH BEATNIK GHOSTS

ROUND 12

@

The Original
SIX GALLERY Site
(Now "KASA")
3115 Fillmore (at Filbert)
San Francisco
6:30 p.m.

Artwork by
Jerry Kamstra
(Shem)

FEATURED PERFORMERS PLUS OPEN MIC

Poets, artists, musicians, mystic boxers and enthusiasts of the spoken word...

Round 13:
SPARRING WITH BEATNIK GHOSTS
@ The Gothic Church Reading

Saturday,
March 19
12;30 p.m.
First Unitarian
Universalist
Church
(MLK Room)
1187 Franklin
(@ Geary) San Francisco

Produced by
D. Yaryan

GUEST HOST
KIRK
LUMPKIN

Latif Harris • Phil Deal • Joyce Jenkins • Sam Sax
Kathleen Wood • Tom Stolmar • Lyzz Bronson • Dee Allen
Special Guests Luke Warm Water and Jennifer Barone
Daniel Heffez on saxophone • Geordie Van Der Bosch on drum

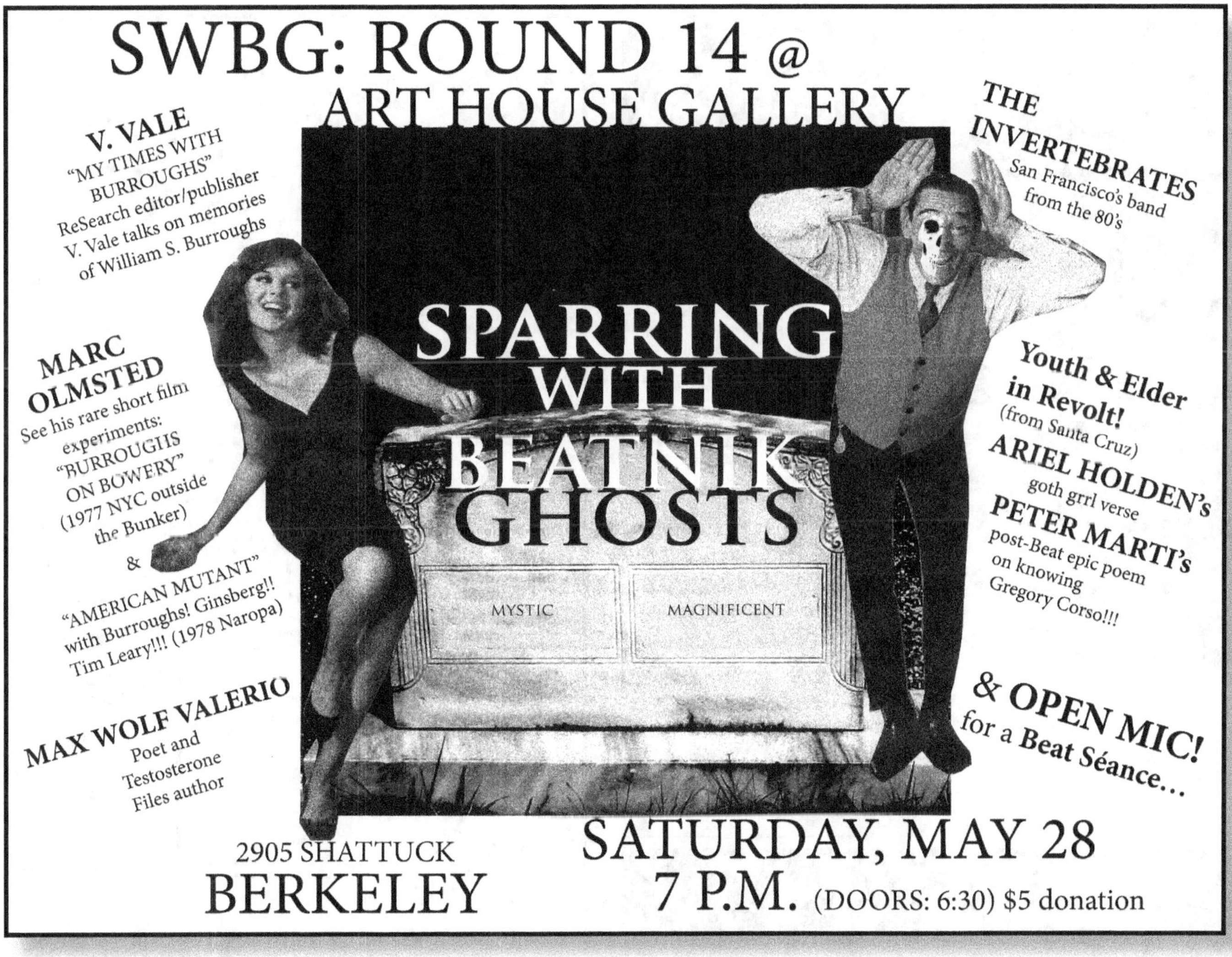

SWBG: ROUND 14 @ ART HOUSE GALLERY

V. VALE
"MY TIMES WITH
BURROUGHS"
ReSearch editor/publisher
V. Vale talks on memories
of William S. Burroughs

**THE
INVERTEBRATES**
San Francisco's band
from the 80's

**MARC
OLMSTED**
See his rare short film
experiments:
"BURROUGHS
ON BOWERY"
(1977 NYC outside
the Bunker)
&
"AMERICAN MUTANT"
with Burroughs! Ginsberg!!
Tim Leary!!! (1978 Naropa)

MAX WOLF VALERIO
Poet and
Testosterone
Files author

SPARRING WITH BEATNIK GHOSTS

MYSTIC   MAGNIFICENT

**Youth & Elder
in Revolt!**
(from Santa Cruz)
ARIEL HOLDEN's
goth grrl verse
PETER MARTI's
post-Beat epic poem
on knowing
Gregory Corso!!!

& OPEN MIC!
for a Beat Séance...

2905 SHATTUCK
BERKELEY

SATURDAY, MAY 28
7 P.M. (DOORS: 6:30) $5 donation

Sparring With Beatnik Ghosts

ANTHOLOGY
OF
SPARRING WITH
BEATNIK GHOSTS ©

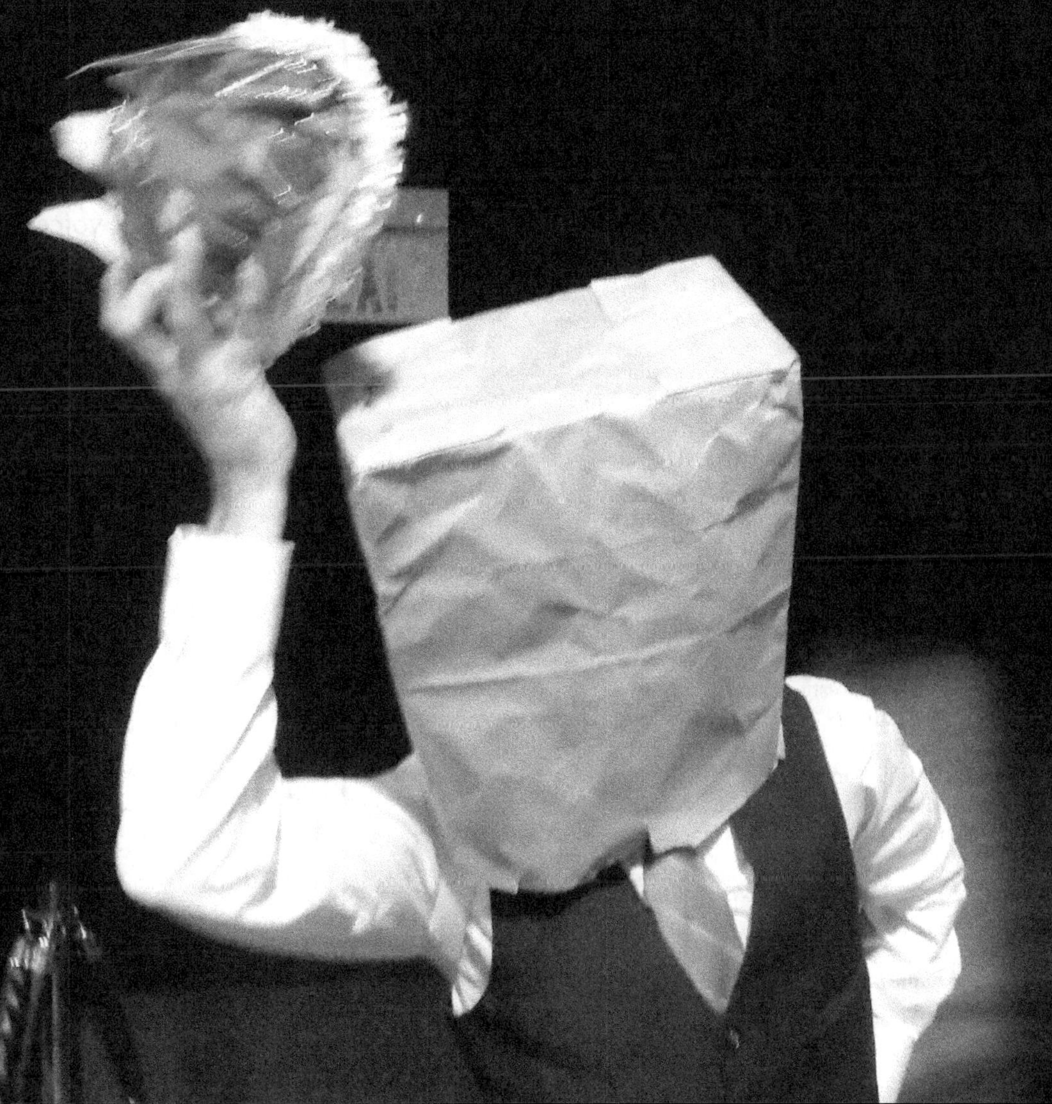

ANTHOLOGY OF

SPARRING WITH BEATNIK GHOSTS ©

Published by:

SPARRING ARTISTS © Daniel Yaryan, 2023
Sparring With Beatnik Ghosts © Daniel Yaryan, 2023

For information, contact Mystic Boxing Commission
Publisher Daniel Yaryan: dyaryan@gmail.com

Editor/Publisher:	Daniel Yaryan
Book Designer:	Yaryan/Peer Amid Press
Special Feature Editor:	S.A. Griffin
Editorial Assistant:	Christy McClain
MBC Staff Artist:	Lynn Rogers
Back Cover Artist:	Mark David Hoefer

Contributing Artists: Tzvi Ben-Aretz, Bob Branaman, George Milo Buck, Margot Chereau, Ann Cohen, Tim Eagan, Stuart Ellis, Alexis Rhône Fancher, Christopher Felver, Fitz, Joe Funk, Bea Garth, Nelson Gary, Jay Green, S.A. Griffin, Sharon Griffin, Lewis W. Hine, Gary Justice, Jerry Kamstra, Karen Kaplan, Luna (TransSurreal Studios), Georges Méliès, Bob Newick, Heather Nova, Lorraine Perrotta, Frank Rios, Lynn Rogers, Egon Schiele, Ella Seneres, Emi Motokawa Sonksen, Daniel Stolpe, Jimmy Townes, T Mike Walker, Marcia Ward, Melissa West, Steven C Wilson, Blair Wilson, Tracy Witt, Hannah Yaryan & Ron Yungul.

ISBN#: 978-1-7335481-6-8
2nd Edition: 9/27/23 – Mystic Boxing Commsion

(1st Edition was limited to 100 copies 9/23/23 –Mystic Boxing Commission)

Photo of Yaryan by Margot Chereau.

ACKNOWLEDGEMENTS

I want to give special thanks to all the wordsmiths and artists who contributed to the *Sparring Artists* anthology, as well as the *Sparring With Beatnik Ghosts* series that these creative individuals participated in — sharing their voices, sounds and visions. Tremendous thanks to S.A. Griffin and Janet Sager Knott for compiling content to share in our tribute to poet Doug Knott — who is highlighted in this special edition. Thanks to Christy McClain, Christopher Felver, Alexis Rhone Fancher, Lynn Rogers, Ella Seneres, Brian Hassett, Mike Sonksen, Marcia Ward, Fitz and Michael C Ford for their creative support of *Sparring Artists*.

An additional shout-out to the back cover artist of this anthology, Mark David Hoefer.

Special thanks to my kids Hannah Yaryan and Andrew Yaryan; and lastly, my eternal gratitude to the late Jerry Kamstra who continues to inspire in many ways, including with the Kamstra Sparchive (Sparring Archive) from where much of this content emerged.

— *Daniel Yaryan*

Sparring With Beatnik Ghosts title and logo
© Copyright 2023 Daniel Yaryan

BRIAN HASSETT
FOREWORD

SPARRING WITH BEATNIK GHOSTS has been transporting people from the present to the coolest past and back again for 15 years! And what's rockin' is — among so many other things — they didn't accept the ancient long-forgotten idea of what 'beatnik' means — and, rather, embrace it in its current usage. I wholeheartedly applaud that, and thus included them in the "Beat vs. Beatnik" webpage that attracts readers from around the world literally every single day. What Daniel Yaryan has been doing in both live shows and publications for so many years has established a quality brand that nobody questions. And it's an honor to include what he's doing along with Diane Di Prima, Helen Weaver, Ed Sanders, The Beat Museum, Vesuvio's, Gordon Ball, Jerry Garcia, Janis Joplin, Donovan, Barack Obama and so many others in recognizing that 'beatnik' is not a bad word.

MIKE SONKSEN
AKA MIKE THE POET
INTRODUCTION

You'd be hard pressed to find anyone who's done more to unite West Coast Poetry than Daniel Yaryan. His Sparring with Beatnik Ghosts readings have included over 90 shows between the Bay Area and LA with one-offs in Santa Cruz, Oakland, Berkeley, and various bookstores and galleries along the coast. Yaryan started his Sparring run at the Li Po Lounge in San Francisco's Chinatown on August 23, 2008. He even hosted a reading at the original Six Gallery where Howl was first read in 1955 on Fillmore in the city.

The new "Sparring Artists (Anthology of Sparring With Beatnik Ghosts)" that you hold in your hands celebrates the 15th Anniversary of the multimedia series with 125 contributors, including a special tribute to Los Angeles poet Doug Knott (of The Lost Tribe and Carma Bums performance troupes).

Almost 500 poets have sparred over the last 15 years including greats like Lawrence Ferlinghetti, Ramblin' Jack Elliott, Wavy Gravy, ruth weiss, Jerry Kamstra, Michael C Ford, Amy Uyematsu, David Meltzer, Lorna Dee Cervantes, Wanda Coleman, Jack Hirschman, Floyd Salas, Lewis MacAdams, Julia Vinograd, Pam Ward & QR Hand. Punk rock, spoken word, jazz, hip hop, surreal, avant-garde, it's all here.

Yaryan's Spars have bridged generations, poetic styles and West Coast poetry. When asked why he started it, he says, "I was compelled to see a legacy of poets live on. This would be done through honoring the living elders and the recently deceased poetic giants. Also, seeing to it that there's a voice for now and into the future. It's important to recognize the past to ensure a new chapter for the artform -- to rejuvenate it and keep it alive."

Read all about it in these pages. Yaryan unites stages, pages and generations of voices in this luminous collection stemming from California but heard coast-to-coast and abroad.

#1

THE SPARRING Artists ©

CONTENTS

Pictured: Doug Knott (with Mike M. Mollett in background, from The Lost Tribe. Photo by JIMMY TOWNES, 1985. See article "Doug Knott, Riverboat Lawyer: A Rememberance" by S.A. Griffin — PAGE 17.

WWW.SPARRINGARTISTS.COM

Mystic Joker by FITZ

SPARRING
SPECIAL
FEATURE
SECTION!

DOUG KNOTT TRIBUTE

EDITED & CURATED BY:
S.A. GRIFFIN

R.I.P. DOUG KNOTT
12/18/43 — 12/23/22

Photo of Doug Knott:
ALEXIS RHONE FANCHER

DOUG KNOTT PRESENTS
SHOW TO GO

EXENE CERVENKA
The Eagle falls from heights unseen
The Angel laughs behind the screen
The Drums of Night delight Exene

FLEA
RED HOT CHILI PEPPER
Bassman Samson busts up Temple of Cool

MICHAEL BLAKE
Personality
Meta-Cowboy wears Stetson of Soul

JAY LEVIN
Editor in Chief, LA WEEKLY
Persuasive Penman means Trouble for Bonzo

THE LOST TRIBE
MIKE BRUNER S.A. GRIFFIN DOUG KNOTT MIKE MOLLETT
Alien Art Gang puts Godzilla Prints at Mann's Chinese

CHERYL TRYKV
Poet Salomé sashays for Subterraneans

Plus

RUDY CABALLERO
Zen improvisationist hears One Hand Clapping

LHASA CLUB
1110 N. Hudson
Thursday **JULY 10**
9pm **Sharp** $6

Doug Knott Presents Show To Go was one af many events produced by Knott in the eighties. Flyer by DOUG KNOTT.

DOUG KNOTT, RIVERBOAT LAWYER: A REMEMBRANCE — by S.A. GRIFFIN

James Douglas Knott, Doug, was born in Richmond, Virginia into a succession of Southern lawyers and judges December 18, 1943. Doug attended both Harvard and Yale (1966), graduating from Harvard Law School in 1971. Inspired by Al Lowenstein, Doug marched at Selma. In 1964 Doug took a year off from his studies to hitchhike around the world via employment on a trans-Pacific Swedish freighter. During the middle of law school (1967-68) he received a Rotary scholarship to study in Rio de Janeiro, Brazil, where he became fluent in Portuguese. Back in the states he made the pilgrimage to Woodstock and knew Richard Alpert (Ram Das). He lived a "hippie life" in Vermont and New Mexico before migrating to Berkeley in 1972 where he entered a Tibetan Buddhist monastery for six months, practicing law as a "new age lawyer" at a storefront in Berkeley, and later in Marin. He began playing rock 'n roll, but lacking the "musical chops" was drawn to the spoken word and poetry movement in Los Angeles during the early 1980s. Much later in life Doug served as the President of the Board of Trustees at Beyond Baroque Literary Arts Center (2013-2019). After being in a relationship with Janet Sager for 13 years, Doug and Janet married in 2014. Doug and his truly beloved Janet relocating to their new home in Ojai a few years ago, remaining together until Doug's passing December 23, 2022 at the age of 79 in Ojai, California.

I first met Doug Knott at the Wednesday night open readings at the Water Espresso Gallery sometime around 1982-83. The Water readings at the time were fairly sedate affairs attended by about 15-20 die-hards. However, those Wednesday nights would soon grow in numbers, blossoming into a wild and dynamic affair attended by the likes of Johnny Forever, Leah Really, Rod (Smear) Sphere, Fish Karma, Johnny Cool, Linda Sibio, Alan Pulner, Mike Maggio and Ben Downing. This was where Doug and I would also meet our other lifelong friends and cohorts in poetic mischief and performance mayhem: Michael Lane Bruner, Bobbo Staron and Mike M Mollett. Very sadly, the Water Gallery would close sometime around 1985, but not before Doug took over the hosting duties during those last months, at times sharing hosting duties with performance poet Leah Really. The Water Espresso Gallery, which rested on the corner of Santa Monica and Hudson, was directly connected to the Lhasa Club and the Figtree Theatre, the entire complex part of a building owned by the artist Frederick Sauls who lived on the top floor. Those were rich and rewarding years, the punk ethos penetrating everything at the time, co-existing with ska, reggae, new wave, mod, techno and performance art. But have no doubt, punk was king! There were few if any venues for us to ply our trade at the time and wanting to break down the walls of conformity

Counterclockwise (front left): S.A. Griffin, Doug Knott, Mike Mollette and Michael Lane Bruner were The Lost Tribe. Photo by JIMMY TOWNES, 1985.

and reach beyond the choir, Michael Lane Bruner, S.A. Griffin, Doug Knott and Mike Mollett conspired to become The Lost Tribe in the back of Mollett's old VW bus. Beginning April 1, 1985, The Lost Tribe performed all over the state of California, but primarily in

CONTINUED NEXT PAGE

and around Southern California. There was no slam poetry at the time, not even a whisper. Even though it may have been on the rise in Chicago, this was the era of phone booths and newspapers. When L.A. was a 24-hour town, long before the madness of 24-hour hamster news on a wheel and endless talking heads bobbing and babbling. There were no computers, no blogs, no texts or tweets, no emails and any calls outside of your immediate area code was long distance, and it wasn't cheap. Nobody knew of anything slam, nobody. And nobody at the time was doing anything like what we had concocted: a four-man well-rehearsed, highly choreographed crack poetry performance ensemble. An atomic fusion of the Marx Brothers, the Three Stooges, a pinch of Busby Berkeley with a healthy dose of THC, Beat poetry and open verse (or worse). We were rock stars with air guitars; an immediate hit.

During this same time period, Doug launched his amazing and truly incomparable Doug Knott Presents (1985-87) at our ground zero, the iconic Lhasa Club, a performance series that often featured not only the Lost Tribe, but a staggering who's who from the period that included such underground and alternative luminaries as Exene Cervenka, John Doe, Henry Rollins, Michael Blake, Dave Alvin, Chuck E. Weiss, Linda J. Albertano, Wanda Coleman, John Densmore, Nina Hagen, Texacala Jones, Keith Morris, The Holy Sisters of the Gaga Dada and Flea. Other highlights for the Tribe included winning the Gong Show with the lowest score ever recorded (8), getting married at Deborah Sweet's fringe wonderland X=Art in West Hollywood (1986), being courted by Late Night with David Letterman at the Improv (for which only Bruner seems to have any memory), opening for Firesign Theater's Peter Berman with our Slobs in Suits act and an original one act play-performance The Tribe Must Be Crazy (1988) directed by the late Scott Kelman for his Pipeline Theatre. The Lost Tribe were also the subject of a short film by John Leslie Foxx, The Lost Tribe, shot on either 8 or 16mm film at the D.A. Ward Studios in the glorious Rose St. building / art lofts, long ago razed and replaced by new world condos and townhouses. All things must pass, and in the present day there is virtually little or nothing left of a once thriving, vital, affordable and grandly symbiotic creative scene. Even in writing this I must remind myself that this all happened 40 years ago, nearly half a century. The mind and creative spirit are always willing, but the forward motion of the world wrapped in time, is not.

The Lost Tribe invitation design by S.A. GRIFFIN.

The Lost Tribe folded in late 1988. In August 1989 we reformed as The Carma Bums with Michael Lane Bruner, Doug Knott, S.A. Griffin, Bobbo Staron and Scott Wannberg as the founding members. Ellyn Maybe was added as an opening act. The following year Bobbo dropped out (and back in a few times) replaced by Mike M Mollett. The Carma Bums was the antithesis of the Lost Tribe, a no-holds barred improvisation swirling around set poetry pieces, described by those who saw us as a "happening", something akin to the infamous Living Theatre. Once again, with no slam influence at all, we were breaking barriers. Nothing we did was ever done as competition

CONTINUED PAGE 20

wed. april 15

We love you.
You're beautiful.
Don't ever change.

dave alvin

wanda coleman

the lost tribe
* MIKE BRUNER * S.A. GRIFFIN * DOUG KNOTT * MIKE MOLLETT *

la loca

bob flanagan

at the

DADALAND WORLD TOUR 1987

lhasa club

1110 n. hudson   461-7284

no age limit

open at 8 p.m.

B.Y.O.

$6
Choose To Be Stupid

Flyer design by DOUG KNOTT and S.A. GRIFFIN.

SHARKTALK DOUGKNOTT

SHARKTALK DOUGKNOTT

SHARKTALK DOUGKNOTT

Knott's first book from Rose of Sharon Press.

The Lost Tribe -- photo by MICHAEL DARE.

CONTINUED FROM PAGE 18
or reward, only as performance in process. For the most part, the Bums toured the U.S. and Canada in my 1959 Cadillac Sedan de Ville Farther. In 1994, The Summer of Natural Born Killers we spent a week at the University of Washington at Seattle to create what was considered the very first poetry website of its kind The Carma Bums International Superhighway Tour of Words, complete with original text and graphics, sound files and hyperlinks. In 1996 we were the subject of a feature length documentary The Luxurious Tigers of Obnoxious Agreement directed by R. Bruce Dickson.

Doug produced hundreds of amazing shows and readings during his lifetime. And as it is said, you can't keep a good man down. Soon after his run at the Lhasa in 1987, together with his partner Shari Famous, he launched another performance series the Famous/Knott Salon, where once again, he tapped into the underground and alternative glitterati entertaining atop the thin edge featuring such incredible acts as the Del Rubio Triplets, counter culture giant Paul Krassner, performance artist Sandra Tsing Loh, NEA 4 superstar John Fleck, and Detective Supremo poet and national treasure Laurel Ann Bogen.

Doug's original one man play Last of the Knotts re-

ceived critical praise for Doug as both author and actor in a successful run as part of the 2011 Hollywood Fringe Festival, enjoying continued success via an extended four year tour which included performances in New York, Winnipeg, West Palm Beach and San Francisco. As an actor, Doug was one of the stars of Bad Day directed by Modi Frank (1986), a comic western shot by Exene Cervenka and co-written by Modi and Exene. The twenty-minute film's stars include Kevin Costner as the town drunk, John Doe as the "tripped-out cowboy priest" and Dave Alvin as the narrator-troubadour. Doug also starred in his own award-winning poetry videos, like his psychedelic, tantric swing through Tinseltown, Sunset Strip Self Improvement Affirmations directed by Joseph Culp.

Doug's first publication, Sharktalk (Rose of Sharon Press, 1988) was followed by Small Dogs Bark Cartoons (Seven Wolves Press, 1991). Other publications include Saved by the Oil Fire (Laguna Poets Series #62, 1997) and Holding Pattern (Laguna Poet Series #122, 1999). Publications with the Carma Bums include Twisted Cadillac (Sacred Beverage Press, 1996) and Armageddon Outta Here! (Rose of Sharon Press, 2004).

Doug's poetry may also be found in Grand Passion:

CONTINUED PAGE 22

Flyer design by MIKE M. MOLLETT and SHARON GRIFFIN.

CONTINUED FROM PAGE 20

The Poets of Los Angeles and Beyond (Red Wind Books, 1995), The Outlaw Bible of American Poetry (Thunder's Mouth Press, 1999), Wide Awake: Poets of Los Angeles and Beyond (Pacific Coast Poetry Series, 2015), Beat Not Beat (Moon Tide Press, 2022) and Sparring With Beatnik Ghosts Omnibus (Mystic Boxing Commission, 2022).

After the passing of our dear brother the electric Scott Wannberg in 2011, marking the end of the Carma Bums, Bruner, Griffin, Knott and Mollett became The Lost Bums creating The Hideous Bible (Rose of Sharon Press, 2015) and a CD Ozark Revelations (Rose of Sharon, 2015). And now, with Doug's passing, we are simply, The Bums.

Doug was more than just a friend; he was my brother. Together as performance partners and poets with our other lost brothers, we suffered the lowest of lows and celebrated the highest of highs travelling thousands upon thousands of miles of discovery together over the decades. A gifted creative, Doug remains one of the most well read, well-traveled and intelligent individuals I will ever meet.

In closing, I leave you with this, the lyrics to a smoking song I wrote for Doug as part of our International Superhighway Tour of Words. I have it on good authority, his wife Janet, that Doug loved this little ditty:

> Doug Knott
> Doug Knott
> Doug Knott riverboat lawyer!
>
> Doug Knott riverboat
> Doug Knott riverboat
> Doug Knott riverboat lawyer!!
>
> D-O-U-G-K-N-O-T-T...
>
> Doug Knott... DOUG KNOTT!!!!

Until we meet again hitchhiking through time... we are, and always will be, dreams and words without end.

High cool. Start from zero.

Love,
S.A.

August 5, 2023
Los Angeles, California

THE CARMA BUMS

Photo by JAY GREEN. Clockwise from left: Doug Knott, Mike M. Mollett, Scott Wannberg, Bobbo Staron (pasted in), S.A. Griffin and Michael Lane Bruner (front, center).

DOUG KNOTT TRIBUTE

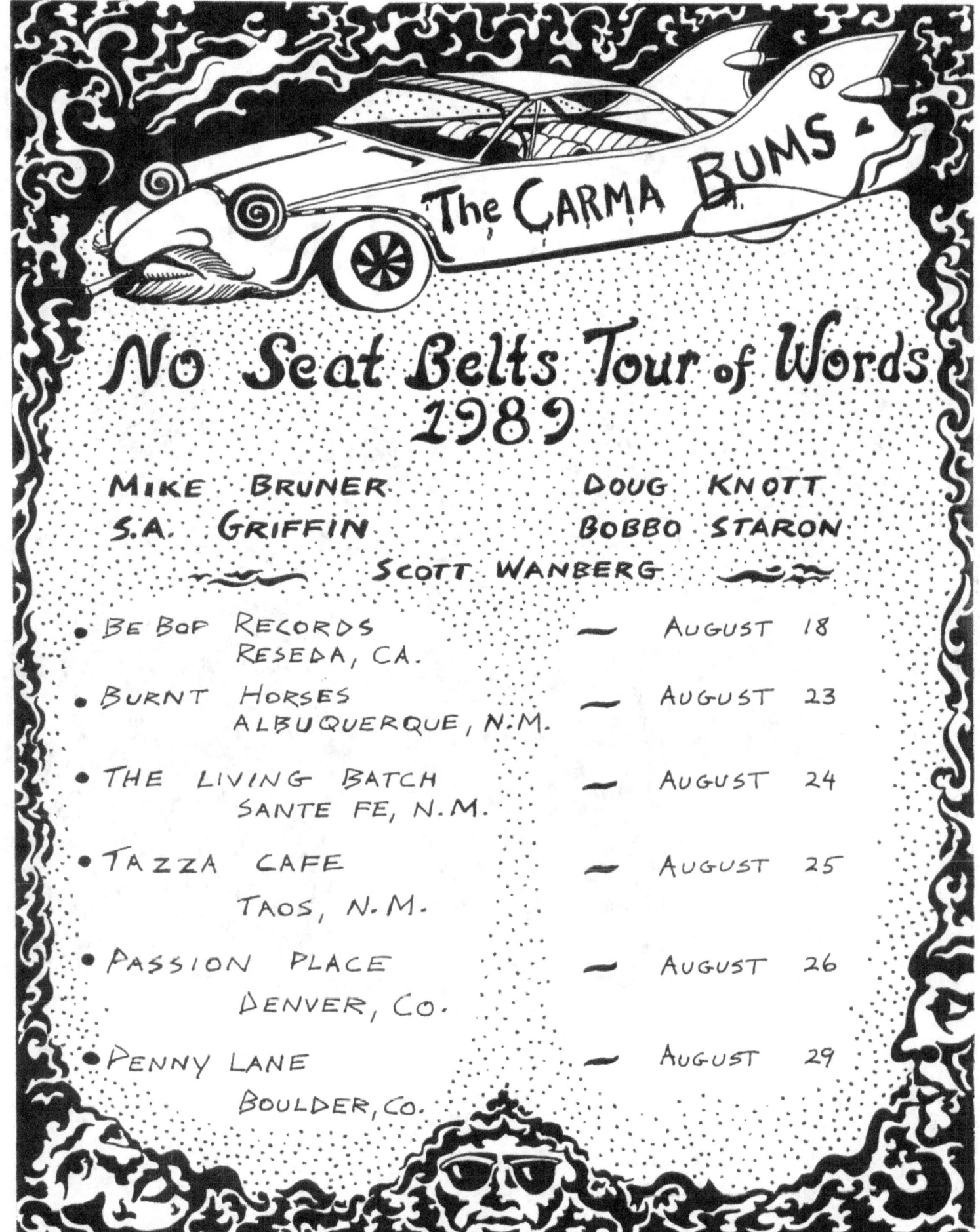

The CARMA BUMS

No Seat Belts Tour of Words 1989

MIKE BRUNER   DOUG KNOTT
S.A. GRIFFIN   BOBBO STARON
SCOTT WANBERG

- BE BOP RECORDS — AUGUST 18
  RESEDA, CA.
- BURNT HORSES — AUGUST 23
  ALBUQUERQUE, N.M.
- THE LIVING BATCH — AUGUST 24
  SANTE FE, N.M.
- TAZZA CAFE — AUGUST 25
  TAOS, N.M.
- PASSION PLACE — AUGUST 26
  DENVER, CO.
- PENNY LANE — AUGUST 29
  BOULDER, CO.

Flyer art and design by STUART ELLIS.

the Lost tribe

March Performances

2nd ed. MM

Sat. March 8 - BeBop Records & Fine Arts Reseda, 9 pm $5
with JODY SWIFT & HANGMAN'S HOLIDAY

Thurs. 13 - Anti Club Hollywood 9:30, $5, with LAUREL ANN BOGEN,
RON KOERTGE, SUZANNE LUMMIS, CHARLES WEBB, NICOLA
MANNING.

Fri. 14 - Laguna Public Library 8pm, 2 bucks only...

Wed. 19 - Gorkys Downtown L.A. • 9 pm, FREE

687-9779
876-8028

Actual values can vary by body-type,
sex, health status, and other factors.

Flyer courtesy of S.A. GRIFFIN. From the KAMSTRA SPARCHIVE COLLECTION.

AN OPEN LETTER TO ME

Doug, deep in the woods,
he squeezed my hand
saying "I'm lost too."

Like a priest, a soothsayer who whispers in your ear,
adding that shock of meaning revealing the truth
in what's false all about us.

Ready to meet death as we must,
our pockets full of cryptocurrencies,
our hero, yes, is down,
down on this lost pirate planet ringed with participatory fruit cake,
where we have all been a lost tribe together:
he and I, and I and us.

Down, he whispers, deep already in the shades:
"It goes back to the trauma of the crib death of my father,
the murderer with the mixed-up mind and
the pistol-whipping Mr. Sun."

"Here in our dreams, we move on wheels upon wheels,
and they are all around us, turning around,"
said the Master of Maxims who soon would not speak for himself,
with a forehead long as death,
an ice cream astrologer who could get things fixed,
if only for a time.

He whispers, if you bend down low enough to hear:
"The earth plane is a storm of triumphs
boiling away our juices,
out into that wonder of our freedom,
and the known world sells us meatballs,
marching across the planet like they own it."

Doug is a Prince on his own beautiful planet,
light as a snowflake,
here among the meatballs
that watch a lot of romance television
that make up what we think life is,
on a truly fake island where nothing happens but palm trees and clouds,
on journeys into the self in a special black bag full of holidays.

He, lying there, cares not who can follow the truths his last breaths allow.

We are bums of karma, ever looking for the signs,
changing our names as we have to,
listening to the endings listening deeply,
wearing our own creative masks
in a world that's a polluted holy place
where they take pictures of your body,
there on the slab.

It's an impossible vision I know.
An open letter to me.
Killer monster chunks of stuff
unleashed for a while and then not.

CONTINUED NEXT PAGE

So go really slow.
Soak it up.
A lot you just have to accept.
It depends upon how far it goes into
a beautiful turn of phrase
we really don't want to destroy.

Whispers, there at our edge,
"Yes, a love story for words."
Words from the ghosts of people, whispering in our ear.
An assonant improv,
all done with horns and pipes through a voice that's not ours.
The art of noise in the form of a riddle,
already wild, and
code talkers from the layered depths in measured fragments of orders
overwhelmed with expectations that would like to sing along.

Then, then, and then again,
the great rollercoaster of reality,
hands held high,
shall be our holy conversation with our internal therapist forever,
here on our high wires looking down into the deep,
in all these forms we are lost in yes
for love.

Poem co-written in memoriam for our lost brother Doug Knott,
by Michael Lane Bruner, Mike M. Mollett, and S.A. Griffin (2023)

DOUG KNOTT TRIBUTE

Flyer courtesy of S.A. GRIFFIN. From the KAMSTRA SPARCHIVE COLLECTION.

WWW.SPARRINGARTISTS.COM

THE CARMA BUMS

1992 LOST TOUR OF WORDS

PRECISION DRILL TEAM POLITICS WITH
THE LOST TRIBE
THE TRIBE MUST BE PRESIDENT OUT OF HISTORICAL NECESSITY.

ELLYN MAYBE
GIGGLING ANGEL WORDSTRESS

CONFRONTATIONAL BRAINAGE AND MADNESS BY
THE CARMA BUMS
MIKE BRUNER, S.A. GRIFFIN
DOUG KNOTT, MIKE M. MOLLETT
BOBBO STARON, SCOTT WANNBERG

AUGUST 13 14 15 AT 8:30 PM
HOLLYWOOD UNITED METHODIST CHURCH
6817 FRANKLIN AVENUE
HOLLYWOOD, CALIFORNIA

AUGUST 16 AT 8PM
RUMOURS CAFE AND COFFEE HOUSE
4994 NEWPORT AVENUE
OCEAN BEACH, CALIFORNIA

ART BY BLAIR WILSON

Art by BLAIR WILSON. Flyer courtesy of S.A. GRIFFIN. From the KAMSTRA SPARCHIVE COLLECTION.

DOUG KNOTT TRIBUTE

DOUG KNOTT
FLANEUR: *LIFE BETWEEN THE CRACKS*

The sky's a breathless blue lung
Central Park's an enormous secret
with grass growing on it

He, almost never she, moves alone
and is happy about that --
amid benches and left-over folk,
their bottles and blankets,
Listening for the tip-toe of the heart

A boulevardier at large enjoys
The pleasure of his very glance
Into life's green planes and flesh-colored angles,
Every gaze, averted or direct, into another's eyes
Is a door into summer or sorrow

A tune grazes his ear
It bursts into a song that then stomps off --
Love is too temporary
To remember those words

He has words, but no apartment
in this boundless city
No roost to cling to.
Where he stays, voices clang.
But he thinks: even a lucky rent-control apartment makes you
A prisoner of this city – where rooftops, watertanks, gargoyles and now video cameras observe even
dog-walkers,
reelers, power-people getting somewhere
lovers hunched against a wall
    And here he is, a butterfly
    Perched on a moment of the impossible
    Sour grapes?
    What peak experience is that?

On a green hillside sits the old emperor
Painting watercolors;
He is alone in a Universe gone green and flat
A static moment of pleasure
The artist remembered when he pulled the world apart --
What a transparency is pain

DOUG KNOTT
THE TANTRIC ORCHARD
for Janet

The Tantric Orchard
I am so lucky to have found this orchard
And you in it
Under the soil our roots embrace
Like small animals driven underground
The twisted branches of the apple trees reach
Back to touch their thighs
Such springtime muscles
Shot off this green cannonball of earth
Lie on the wet grass with me
Like fruit we swell and rub against each other
Kiss like raindrops in the milky sunlight
Grasping roots inside you
I will transplant them in a shrine
Alive with wet green dripping things
That shake themselves awake
And I will visit you with blue lakes and reckless hills
And we will watch the large white birds fly by
Like abandoned opportunities searching for their season
Around us, black grappling branches orchestrate the air
which parts, and endlessly parts again
The whole orchard ripples in a soft green chord
Where the land ends, and the feelings begin

Art by *DANIEL O. STOLPE.*

DOUG KNOTT
THE AWARE WOLVES

To the aware wolves belong
The space between ghosts
And night of eggplant dark

The moon, itself a wandering soul,
Peers through tree-tops
At my heart – a deer frozen
In a forest of eyes, lupine
And shaped like leaves

I know they are near
I hear them when they call
My name. Summoning me
Is entertainment
At my own expense

They lope alongside me
And when I look at them
Their eyes get bigger

I treat them now as my children
Feed them everything I have.

And at night I draw these friends around me
and look up at the moon
Awash in darkness, and hunger is
A long wail in the night

DOUG KNOTT
GRAMPIE WORE GRAY
(Orig: "Grandfather in St. Augustine is Gone"   --Doug Knott Rev 9-10-21)

He was the coolest guy
Gave me a little bicycle when I was 6
which I learned to ride on the stone path around
The grand old Spanish fort, its walls 30 feet thick,
later occupied by English invaders,
and then the militant Confederacy --
the best fort ever for a little boy!

Grampie played a card-game
Called Russian Bank with 4 decks
And two players, and when I played with him
He remembered every trick
And hid behind his fan of cards,
murmuring, "bad, bad, bad"
and then nailed me with his hidden Queen, of course --
So I appreciated his military technique

His own father a lieutenant in the Confederate Army
His father's father, a private in the same,
My grandfather was proud of the Army of Northern Virginia
And made sophisticated jokes about President Lincoln,
pointed out the battles, like Chancellorsville
And Olustee just out of Jacksonville
where "we done beat the Yankee" and
killed 500 Union soldiers
200 of whom were black

But my grandfather was buddies with an old black guy
Named Singleton, who rode a bicycle
and fixed things around the house
They cruised around together side by side
in the wide front seat of grandfather's old Cadillac;

But on my dad's side, my uncle in Tallahassee
Threw me out of the house after I did the big Selma march in '65 -
Said I stunk like the N-word
But I was glad to go

And left Dixie and the Lost Cause to go to school
Up North in Yankeeland where they called me "South'ner,"
so I dropped my cracker accent to fit in
and even said I was from New York, New York, and started
Talking like I was Jewish from Brooklyn; and then
the South got real un-popular
But I was in the Civil Rights generation
marching in the big marches because I thought it was right
And became a beatnik type of modern person

Although I am no longer modern,
But peeking over the edge of my personal world
As it extends day-to-day and flat like a map,
which means I will soon fall off the edge
Into "here be dragons & sea monsters"

Photo by LEWIS W. HINE

And it looks like the Confederate Army has come around again
Now flying the banner of the criminal ex-president
Except without the bravery, dignity and honesty
Of my grandfather --

And I know how they think: that they got screwed
and will stand tall and fight back against invaders,
And how tough they are, and how much they love the orange-haired demon
Who spews insect lies to inspire their fierce Cause, now Lost,
They are the most righteous form of man

And they will not respond to peace
Because they are accustomed to casual hate,
Like the chewed cigar gone sour in the bowl

And I see them on the other side of me
Like Arjuna, the mythical prince of India
saw his own family rigged out and carrying swords
On the enemy side in the "Bhagvad Gita;"

But I don't ride in Krishna's stone chariot of mind;
I ride my mental bicycle around a lucky fort called home
And my grandfather is 50 years all bones
In the disintegrating swamp of history
With his battle-winning cards from the game of Russian Bank,
Sentimental affection for the Stars and Bars,
And a little boy's love;

He's all fermented in his box under the Spanish moss,
the verdant stink of the salt marshes
always near the nose in St. Augustine
sweat even in the shade

and now only a memory
a movie about to end,
that little bicycle rolling downhill
through the last bars of the ancestral song
"In Dixie land where I was born,
look away, look away"
Richmond, Virginia, 1943
Going, going,
and gone

YOUSSEF ALAOUI
Pages from a longer story called…
THE CHEST OF OPEN SCROLLS

The family should be back shortly. I must have frittered enough time chasing my imagination around the house. Maybe I should get out front and wait for them to return. How… Let's see, how might that be possible? I really just want to slide open one of the windows down here. But none of them will open. The back door is paned glass and wood. I can probably break one of the panes using the towel to protect my hand. Or, I could use a rock. That's good. First, wait out front, just in case. I hop over the short wall, neglecting the small gate, and walk around to the street. The front of the house and garden are enclosed in their own tall fortress-like wall. I need to open the outside gate, but it's locked solid. No. I don't want to deal with it. I go back. They'll return to find one small pane of glass missing in the back door. That's it. They'll understand. It would be the least of their worries. I'll have to do it quick and clean and sweep up so the kids don't get hurt. Okay that's the new plan. I find a fist sized rock from behind the house, go in through the small gate, grab one of my towels, and with certainty and compunction, I knock the pane of glass nearest to the inner door handle. It falls out whole and crashes into splinters when it hits the clay tile floor. I'll clean that right away… I reach in, unlock the knob, cut my hand and wrist, bleed, and hold it with the towel. Now there's blood on the back door and the bath towel. I run to the kitchen to rinse off and tie a kitchen towel around my wrist and hand. I belt some cognac from the bottle and look for a broom. Aha. There's a short broom and dust pan by the stove.

As I pass the bank of couches, I notice the body is gone. They finally returned; I suppose. I quietly hustle to clean every bit of glass and pour it into the kitchen garbage. I run and make sure to get the finest sharp grains by the door. I walk back to the kitchen and pour it into the trash. "Hello?" No answer. I walk through the house; I look in every room and bathroom upstairs. I put my blazer on. I look out front. No one is here… not even the body. Do cadavers walk? No, but they certainly sit up. I sit by the fire and stare into it. There's no body. How could I lose the body? It's now oddly scaring me that there is no body. I should be afraid of something I do see, rather than something I am not seeing… right? I have no idea anymore. I check under the couches. Nothing. No wonder they needed someone to watch the body! Does this… *happen* from time to time here? I pour myself another cognac in the kitchen and come back to the fire and watch it for a good long time. The house is quiet. The wind is quiet. The waves are quiet. The moon has begun its descent over the silver ocean. There is nothing I can do at this point. For the first time in almost 20 hours, I allow my eyes to close.

I'm awakened with a start not long after. It sounds like an explosion inside the house. I swivel my head to look for the source. It's still dark. I rub my eyes to witness an unholy scene so terrifying that I believe my heart stops for a moment. I grasp my chest and tremble violently, sweat oozing from my pores. I see the moon, hovering large and low, seemingly near to the house, interfering with the night and suspended by the fog like a heavy balloon, casting a silvery light over the ocean, the rocks, and spilling all over the back terrace, but the sight is blocked beyond the small gate that opens to the cliffs by none other than the silhouette of Kadir's body in his flowing white djellaba covered by the sheet, hovering upright in front of a bonfire that is taller than his person, with long slow flames that lick a swarm of sparks floating into the night sky. I fall to my knees before the window and peer out, too frightened to go outside, hiding out of sight, fearing for my life. On every flat edge of rock, surrounding the scene and headed out to the water, creatures of the deep, every kind imaginable, writhe with tentacles and tails squirming in the air, grasping at the moon. I swallow down hard, gulping what I fear to be another attack of beetles, or maybe its an acid belly caused by the cognac. I wipe at my eyes and forehead and look again. It is all still there. My nerves are shredded after everything that has happened. I have no idea what to do. Could this all be the most heinous prank a student has performed on their professor? But, how could the sea creatures be complicit?

My reactions of fear and confusion transform into a kind of blind rage. I throw open the back door and I tackle the hovering body, flop it over my shoulder, and haul it back inside. The lights of the house react to what I'm doing by strobing in a swirling pattern throughout every room, on every wall. I'm dizzy and losing balance, but I still have a grip on the body over my shoulder. I slam and lock the back door behind me as I stand behind the bank of couches. He was too vulnerable there on the couch. I must find another place to secure his body. Every single door and window in the house trembles. Kadir's corpse seems to be undergoing a form of supernatural attack. I must keep the body contained somehow. I suppose I could tie it to the table and lock him up in the dining room. There is a set of double doors that connect to the living room and another in the front hall. It's the only room in the house that does not have a window. I flop Kadir on the long oval table and light the buffet candles. I throw a sheet over him. The dining room doors all fly open and then slam shut, trapping me inside with him. The candles are extinguished. It is absolutely dark. I tug and tug but the doors do not open. Every other door in the house rattles spastically and the wind chimes clang in a frenzy, as if they are about to smash themselves. I light a candle and hold it overhead.

One by one, the chairs from around the table are swiped away by an invisible force. Kadir trembles, then shakes wildly as deep laughter increases throughout the room. All the doorknobs of the house sound as if there's a person on each one frantically trying to get in. I do my best to hold him down. Might he actually be alive? But his skin is still a putrid green. It makes the hair on his face and neck look thick and stark. I set the candle down. Then I notice some kind of disruption forming deep in his torso. It seems like something alive is desperate to escape and racing circles under his djellaba. In frustration, I rip it open and throw back the sheet. His face stretches into an elongated scream and the eyes droop open yellow, with bright veins crackling at the edges. Deep bellows come from the walls of the dining room. With my hands, as carefully as I can, I try to calm the body. I smooth the skin of the chest but my hands sink into it. Something is squirming deep in the flesh and as I retract in disgust, I pull out a blood drenched scroll with thick calligraphy on it. It's rough writing and the paper is soaked deep red, if only I could read Arabic! As I examine it, more scrolls emerge. They continue, mounding underneath my palms, overflowing the table in soggy, bloody piles with clots of flesh. As more come out, now they are somehow dry. They pop up to fill up the air and fall in piles on the floor beneath. I can't hold them back. They're going every which way. I give up my efforts, sobbing, and stand back. The body calms its seizure. The chest cavity lays pulpy and empty. I am standing in piles of blood and flesh and many, many scrolls, all over the room.

A voice screams in the walls with a wretched, wheezing stress upon it saying, "I was always going to be a writer just like you! Yes! Even better than you! You are so easy to beat, Larousse! You tried to destroy me with your snide self-righteous European literature! My writings are broader than the mountains, vaster than the fields, more pure than spring flowers, made of humanity itself! You'll never live beyond this, Larousse. You are doomed!"
"What are you talking about? Is this some kind of practical joke? I don't have time for this kind of chicanery. Come out of there right now, wherever you're hiding!"

"Ohhhhhhh I'll show you where I am hiding. I am in your heart! I am in your mind! I am the blood in your veins and the beetle in your belly! I am Morocco. I am Maghreb. I am Africa!"

TZVI BEN-ARETZ

TZVI BEN-ARETZ is an Israeli American artist. In his youth, he studied art at Renanim School in Tel Aviv. After his military service, Ben-Aretz studied at the Art Institute in Bat Yam and the Bezalel Academy of Art and Design.

Ben-Aretz won a scholarship from the America-Israel Cultural Foundation and a Ford Foundation grant. He earned his MFA at Pratt Institute in New York.

Ben-Aretz creates mixed media paintings, works on paper, installations and live body projects. He exhibited in numerous shows at museums, galleries and public exhibition spaces throughout the United States, Israel, Ireland, Italy, Portugal, Holland, Germany, Mexico, Turkey, Poland and Russia. His live body installations were in the United States, Israel and Turkey. Ben-Aretz received several newspaper reviews including the *New York Times, Art Forum* and *Flash Art* magazines.

Tzvi Ben-Aretz also performed in the Israeli Opera, movies and commercials.

Email: tzvianartist@yahoo.com

TZVI BEN-ARETZ "To Sacrifice" Live Body Installation at Bat Yam Museum, 2012

TZVI BEN-ARETZ "A Mourning" from the Sacrifice Series Live Project at Performance Arts Platform, Tel Aviv, 2005

TZVI BEN-ARETz "An Altar" Live Corner Installation, Gallery on the Cliff, Netanya, Israel, 2002

"Full Tank of Fuel" **photo by DANIEL YARYAN**

IRIS BERRY
PORTRAIT OF MY LOS ANGELES…

It's the earthquake weather in me
It's my love for palm trees
and the way they line certain streets.

My love for supermarkets
with their big empty parking lots.

It's taking long drives
through various canyons.

It's being in love with
certain silhouettes and views
of trees and telephone poles
as the sun sets
because I've seen them
all my life
and they're embedded in my soul.

It's having love for certain streets
because they have no sidewalks.

It's my ability to love the ocean
only through a restaurant window
but disliking it with its direct Sun
if asked to lay in it
scantily clad
for more than 2 minutes.

It's my love for the stars
the ones in the sky
and on sidewalks.

It's growing up with an empty backyard
but having to drive far
to visit friends and family.

It's only knowing the changing seasons
by what's on display
on the shelves at the supermarkets.

It's having to drive everywhere
just to get anywhere.
It's being bummed when it rains

even though there's a drought.

It's talking on the phone with friends
more than seeing them in person.

It's my love for the beach
but rarely seeing it.

It's being guilty of saying,
it's hot but it's a dry heat.

It's refusing to go somewhere because,
I probably won't find a place to park,
and yet there are parking lots everywhere.

It's all the famous streets and boulevards
with their incredible history.

It's many different cultures
and subcultures and cults.

It's the place where people
come to *Be Somebody*.

It's definitely a love/hate thing.
Sometimes it's like the greatest drug
and the best place on earth
and sometimes it's like telling someone
you love them and they don't say it back.
But it's my home
I was born here
I can't imagine
living anywhere else
I can't imagine
leaving Los Angeles…

Iris Berry … 1/27/23 Midnight…

AVA BIRD
MANY YEARS

many years
 many moons
ago
maybe not
so
 long ago
and far away
those days of energy
and sunshine
 those days of sliding and surfing and skating
late nights
and now
it's all something else
entirely
 now
even though
 those days still live
in the hallways, the albums, the videos, the tapes
the shapes of all the memories
still alive
in the kitchens
the hearts still on shelves
sitting
urns and albums
and wedding bells still sound
down the hall
the bedrooms
the kitchens
of creations

memories
moving
the new generations
progress, change
coming up
yet
coming back to the basics
the simple things
chop wood, carry water
 gardens
of beginners' mind
finally
floating, swimming, dreaming
the soil and dirt and water
 playing with the earth
again
me
in the gardens
of lives
backyards
back in time
freely
deeply
purely
laughing
over
all
these years

LAWRENCE BERGER
POLITICS IS GETTING BETTER!

The primary season is upon us again
but this time there's a twist:
No Democrats allowed!
No Republicans allowed!

Only Working Families can vote.
Who knew there was actually a
Political Party for Working Families?
Apparently, the town elections board did!

I felt bad, I got turned away from voting because I'm single.
Only working Families could vote.
No Libertarians allowed!
No Green Pary allowed!
Just hard-Working Families of Americans!

I had trouble seeing on the short ride home
My eyes were filled with tears of Joy.
I felt proud to be an American again!
Politics is getting better!

LEE BOEK
I WOKE UP ONE MORNING

I woke up one morning completely down in out.
Sleeping in a garage
Rats
Nobody loves me
Nobody cares
Could it be all the bones on my walls?
The man says, "Everything plays out."
I say, "Time to be elsewhere."
A Ford Fairlane for fifty bucks
I drive it up from under ground
My buddy Harald, he slips me a "C" note
Just to get me outta town
Yeah, he still loves me but thinks it a good idea
I get outta here
A.S.A.P.
And that's when I headed for Los Angeles.

Lee Boek photo by Christopher Felver

LAUREL ANN BOGEN
JONAH AT FIVE MONTHS

Wiggling sprig, let the world
wind up its delight machine

You newfangled sprout
You sloppy kiss
You whirling carousel
                of abundant shebang

All is yes and exclamation!

Who can deny you?

Not the wind -- humming
its lullabies in your ear at night

Or that October sun
waiting for you each morning
all butterscotch and honey

Let it spill
         over
ooze
gold laughter
        and joy
            sweet
                sweet joy

LAUREL ANN BOGEN
UKRAINE, 2022

The haggard man
still stands
raises his fist
spits, roars back
at the rutting
threat two
three four times
larger

under God
with justice and liberty
is no small feat

the unsuspected threat
the push-over with steel core

plow us down and again
we rise
weeds
common as breath

LAUREL ANN BOGEN
IN THE PLACE BUT NOT OF IT

Within the silence
of the past but not
of memory: desire

I call out
speak to me

and wait in the silence
for more silence
no echo
but palpable
darkness surrounds
me with webs hidden
from sight

part of this place
but not of it

the distant pinprick
of transfigured light
narrows through caves
of my own making
there is no happiness
in this --

unaware of self
let go the wounded self

"Quizzical Heart" art by BEA GARTH

JIM BOLT
SWEET SCIENCE

You're my Frazier
I'm your Ali

You hit me with blows that could knock down a wall
Knock down my walls

I got combinations you ain't never seen
You got rhythms that could power a metropolis or two
We got a dynamo that could power a millennium or two

This dynamic like
What-It-Is What-It-Is What-It-Is
Is
Feinting and weaving
Light on our feet
Dancing around the edges

Of our
Inevitable
Unseen
Main Event

Like the
Well-heeled
Well-trained
Well-matched
Practitioners of this Sweet Science
We have longed to call our own

Until tonight
Until the roar of this crowd
Is drowned out by the silence of our
Do-Or-Die
All-At-Risk
One-Way-Out
No-Holds-Barred
Flurry of personal exchanges

Don't take it personally
Take it into your dreams
Take it to the mountaintop
Take it, Baby
Take my Word for it

Makes me proud
The way you
Stand up to me
Like for once
I got a game
That won't

Play games
I got a match
With no catch
I got a mirror
That just gets
Clearer and clearer
That won't break

And no matter what I give
You can take it
And make it
Refract
Rays of glistening
Pearlescent light
Fanning out
Like a bejeweled peacock

Beyond the call of Beauty
Into the Sweet Science of Revelation

So no more shadow-boxing, OK?
I can't see your face in these shadows

Step into my ring
Step into my lights
Step into my Sweet Science

And go a few rounds with me...

MATTHEW BOWERS
BEAT CHILD

Beat Child Beat Child Running wild
Through the streets Raw Emotion
Full of heat pounding to the beat
Against the wall standing tall
And I follow her to the end of time

Slippery wet Silhouette
Your name and number tattooed on mind
Lest I forget this moment in time I believe

Pin Eyed girl porcelain skin
I never knew who's dream I was in
Clara Bow style double agent smile
I always looked both ways
Before I crossed That street

Maybe you don't remember
I know I'll never forget
The dancing the cocktails
The darkness… regret

The sun always burned
In the night we came to life
You punctured my heart
With a switchblade knife

Beat Child Beat Child Running wild
I follow her to the end of time

JACK BOWMAN
SUNDAY WARP DRIVE

Frank sits in the living room watches old sci-fi with Michael Rennie

a lesser-known classic from '66, climax with a fist fight in a ghost town

a time jump

he remembers the cars in the road scenes,

he gets a call,

has to go drive his Mother in law's car some distance,

road trip, the battery had died, just got a jump,

he heads up to the high desert

Aqua Dulce and back

part of him just wants to keep going, an adventure, a few old characters

a time jump

he goes home,

finishes the movie

feels like a ghost town.

JACK BOWMAN
SEEING NEW JULY

New faces in transparent dust

wings of glass fly by

make his eyes follow them through medium blue skies of today

while tomorrow lies behind a series

of grey compacted walls of cloud

that sit and wait their turn

until the giant yellowed moon passes, rises up,

beyond three weathered palms

on the eastern horizon.

BOB BRANAMAN
I JUST BROKE UP WITH A VAMPIRE

All the leaves were falling
Everything fades velvet
Purple and mahogany
Wine and gold
O the teenage soul
I just broke up with a vampire
She didn't want my soul
So now the days
Are dark and faded gray
Lingering thoughts
Of the poppies song
The ancient scripts
And bloody trips
The memories fade
My mind is rice
I'm walking besides a creek
It's filled with ice
I won't kid you now
It's not nice
The vampires gone
But the werewolf's
Are tiring to come

BOB BRANAMAN
(UNTITLED)

I don't even know what day it is
I seem to be coming apart
My mind, my body, my art
The computer's starting to fritz
The love life fizzled
Out
I am ready to kill it
I won't even will it
Just let it fall
Letting go of it all
I sit in the back yard
Trying to be empty
The apple tree, big bougainvillea
Gentle fig tree and flowers
The humming birds and bees
Crows and fleas
All just taking care
Of the Void

"Mysterious Conjunction" art by BOB BRANAMAN

BOB BRANAMAN
TUESDAY, JULY 04, 2006

Everyone is out
lighting their fire crackers.
I'm starting to get over my cold
and her.
I feel like my ol' self,
Sort of lonely,
Unappreciated,
and fuckin' ornery as hell.
Mother Fucker,
I'm gonna go out and get some.
I mean dinner,
maybe a movie,
or a quick cruise
of Barnes and Noble.

LYNN BRONSTEIN
ALIYAH

Come, take my hand and walk with me
To the corner and up the hill.
Do you see that garden, with the colorful blossoms?
It isn't far. Don't be afraid.
We can get there. If we trust that we can.

We look into each other's eyes and see
How different we are.
Just as there are so many colors in the garden's flowers,
We are two of those colors
That the grown-ups say divide us.

We make the climb anyway.
Stumbling over recently dislodged earth,
Giggling at our efforts, we finish our journey,
Pulling at each other's arms until we reach the gate.
You bow to your angels
And I say the Holy Words.
We breathe in air with a scent
Like honey
And wish that we could bottle it
And take it back to our friends, so they'd know
On this day, we made Aliyah.

Art by KAREN KAPLAN

JEFFREY BRYANT
THIS POEM CONTAINS SMOKING, LANGUAGE, NUDITY AND SEXUAL SITUATIONS

I'm at this movie that contains language,
dripping out of every lip-sticked mouth,
girls inhaling guys then exhaling them into cuffs.
It's got sinister sisters in violent shadows, and boys
eye shadowing boys.
This movie has language like heat,
which some girl keeps in her purse just in case,
and just in case always comes around
and tells her to hand it over. Language,
languid and lurid, tumbling out and
into every freshly made bed of peril,
scented sheets, silk, stretching out like bodies upon
bodies like an orgy or a war. Bodies landing in fatal arms,
girls falling into girls breathing in each other,
grown men lasting as long as they can until the cops, the kicks,
the cars, the crash, the cocks, the fucks, and the shits
language crisp and sharp as any switchblade pressed against a vein.
This movie with all the bad girls bumming your last smoke,
and the pretty boys who love to lick danger off the spoon.
Then some guy,
some mug, acting all blue-eyed and good-for-nothing,
pushes down a seat next to mine, to laugh where I laugh,
at all the language and the smoking and the sexual situations, and he
sticks his hand down into my popcorn and we get up
to make a movie at his place, butter still warm on our fingers,
rubbing language out of each other until we fade out,
and he lights up,
saying nothing,
nothing at all, and then we fall asleep,
nude, extinguished, spent, mute.

MICHAEL LANE BRUNER
MONKEY MASK

Start the day so you can find an illustrated catalogue of information from a treasury of honest restrictions that unfold really while all eyes are on half price so you can save a lot on a look across what's coming in this great volume of pictures that demonstrate as never before how there is nothing better after a magnificent light on the spot we call home.

Our poor slums contain the faintest stages of a nuclear blast where a different kind of national valentine tells you how the finished go to waste because there is nothing new to tell yourself.

Go still to talk with circumnavigators after dining on the bombing of where we're from in life as it is when you follow unfamiliar faces to help forget all of the kinds of harm we cause and to feel like we have known it all along even if our own years of flight can't find a real cure.

Collage Poem from *To Learn More Visit*, 2021

"In the Beginning" art by BOB BRANAMAN

REX BUTTERS
WHO'LL BE THE FIRST
TO TRY TO SELL THE SPOT
WHERE HE DROPPED?

his flame tipped
sunkist dreadlocks
framed the positive vibration
grin
no saint/thank gods
just trying to beat the odds
sell some incense and stay clean
"blessed!"
he'd respond to "how's it going?"
rebuilding the life
he almost lost
now lived one day at a time
suddenly
soulless suits and their pandering political puppets
declared selling incense and oils a crime
he tried to jump
through the city's arbitrary hoops
dance to the changing tune
subject to unjustified
       unwanted
        unfair regulation
doors shutting too fast
the bottle reopened
mounting pressures
blew a small vein
in his brain
dead on the boardwalk
denied livelihood by the city
another gentle soul
plowed under
more greed machine grease
even the jaded bitch whore Venice
once a goddess/now merely a celebrity
looks away in shame

he'd say
     "hey Rex
     saw your new one
     in the Beachhead!
     Alright!"

this time, Cecil
it's about you
but you're not here
to read it

"Unknown Image" art by DANIEL O. STOLPE

DON KINGFISHER CAMPBELL
DREAM ROOMS

(1)
Darkness arrives,
we take off our eyes,
lock mouths,
wrap limbs,

become two
puzzle pieces
on the bed.

(2)
Hamsters in the box
with a cut-out window,
huddling close

impressing love
on each other's body.

(3)
I hug
my decade-long duende.
She strokes the hair
of her incubus

wishing
nine lives.

(4)
Trucks pass,
phantoms
down the street.

We might as well be
on a coupon vacation
at a Dana Point Super 8.

(5)
We breathe in waves
under seaweed sheets,
mussles undulating
on percale beach.

We toss and turn
in the flotsam and jetsam
of separate but equal
dream worlds.

(6)
Lying at this moment,
other apartments
do what we have done,

moan exercise as people
imitate sleep.

(7)
If an earthquake comes,
we won't watermelon mind.

We'll just hold on
ready for evaluation
preferring mutual breakage.

(8)
But the sun rises.
Our minds return
to conscious light,

twitter
conversation relay,
door departure.

(9)
Until we meet
again in the night,
the nocturnal creatures,
yin and yang,

two familiar
with being endangered.

"The Changling" collage art by T. MIKE WALKER

JUAN CARDENAS
THE BEAT OF AN ANGEL

Holy are the hearts
Of the eyes that see a brother and sister in everyone
Their beats the music that spin the wheels of peace

The Beat needs no flag
Waving through our skies
only the wings of our grandfathers

Resilient
the beat dreams
But never sleeps
The sun their Halo
The moon their blanket
Theirs the earth caressing their feet

Angels Through the downtown's skyscrapers,
petal scented, bright skin shoes clicking with echo

Angels on Freeway tunnels,
knobless doors,
stomach rumbling in echo,

Angels all of them
The rich and the poor angels
Angels show who is the weirdest angel
On a sofa eating popcorn,
Zippin on holy water,
laughing at what we call Angels,

The beat of the angel's congested veins
Slows down as the
powerless wings attempt to lift the heavy giant

Hand tight embracing the lighter
He lit the future
And as it engulfed away
So did himself

JESSICA M. WILSON CARDENAS
BRING A KATANA TO A KNIFE FIGHT

When I think of a spar,
I think of a word war, back and forth until one falls to the floor,
tongue tied out over the dirty drawers laid out without remorse.

When I think of a spar,
I think of the tally from a classroom discussion:
> *"Well what did they mean by that?"*
"What's more important, your instincts or capitalism?"
> *"Who thinks we need money?"*

Nothing but a whisper until one kid calls out,
dying to come along for the ride, yells out, *"Timber!"*, to the teacher,
who motions the youth along for another mind melt of discovery.

No, let's go to the store and take back the eggs.
The yolk runs too thin and exploits all the letters on my plate so they stand out in the moonlight.
There's no alphabet sure enough
to spar back the anecdote to a less miserable way to earn a living.
Anecdotal variety - a vacation that lends itself to too many hands,
only to hold the dollar bill casually until it's ripped
into strips.
A cutup of the smile that wore hope in the blue of the afternoon.
A bow tie clipped right under the shag
of hipped out hair,
diggin for a debt of understanding.

Let's spar under the sheet
of casual sex.
A sway of the blanket, bulging over your hips.
It's more flattering that way.
Pull the sheet back just enough to see your skin peeling;
burnt layers from the sun's seed.
These rays that simmer into the tapestry
of your poem.
A relief from the karma
shoving back into the musk.
The light will fade from its intention.
The ink will swell out in good sweat
until your lips are unrecognizable words
thrown around in
one night stand
bed stand.

A think duty to tuck away
beyond the meaning
of heavy lust.
> - Jessica M. Wilson August 14, 2023
> - 808pm

PETER CARLAFTES
MAN
KNOWS
NOTHING

all I was
was just a guy —there
working at this bar

pouring beers
and mixed drinks
dreaming —that
the roses
would soon bloom
around the thorns
of should've-beens,
and all the stems of
what I'm-gonna's.

on most days
first through door
would come
this unromantic couple

He —Her boss;
Him of cheap suit
(married elsewhere).
She — much taller.

They'd sit —nursing
two white wines
across a table
in the corner,

exchanging looks
in silence;
He would fidget.
She would smile.

and then —about
the time or so
their wines were
mostly done,
she'd put her hand
upon his knee

caressingly
then blush.

this tired act
three times a week
for 6 or 7 months,
until —one night, I realized
they'd gone missing
(no great loss).

unlike that job,
then —soon, a marriage.
living means
to finite end...

finding me sometime later
with a shit job at a blues club,
standing outside —on the street
staring at 2 frenzied women
in the front seat of a car,
and I mean —necking
like I'd never seen before.

then I noticed the one
on the passenger side
was the knee-stroking babe
from the bar
and when she got out
she shot me this look—that
smacked earth off its axis
(like) a man don't know
jack- cumming-shit
'bout pleasing but the self,
and —there beyond the premise
that the girls know more than boys,
I realized pleasing others
comes to human foible naught
so the only worth remaining —lies
these words please someone else.

MONA JEAN CEDAR
BENT KEROUAC

Beats Bend as Circuits Swing Sound Strange
Cacophony funny Noise Plays Poetry Sweet Tweet
Twiddle dee dum Drum Beats blow blues Jazz Bent
Sent into the Awaiting Air Arriving on Ready Ears
  What's that Music mean? Going round & around in
Circus Circuit Sounds   Wailing long low loose blues
  Be Bops Up Beat rhythm & Blues Choose – Sad
Soulful muse of the melancholy Melodies or Hip Slick
Sassy Tunes to tap toes, snap fingers bob head- It's all
there – in between the notes – in the Silence, deafening
delusional   Swinging ever onward Stringing you
along for the ride of a moment- marching meandering
– halting only for effect only to tumble on again –
forward like time & tide taking you with it. Where?
  Does it matter? It'll never be here again – But right
now it's here. You're here – We're all Here Hearing tis
crazy song feeling friends   keeping time along side-
inside this music moment in time - Enjoying this
Joyful Noise. Peace

NEELI CHERKOVSKI
ARCHIVE

that I might find you
behind the wheel of a pale green Porsche
or in the land wild
composing on an Underwood typewriter
in a messy East Hollywood bungalow
ferreting-out the ghost of birdwatcher
hiking mountains in the clouds
dismissing snow warnings

I'm sent a catalogue of my papers
and peruse it at road's end

I might identify
the kid wandering Hollywood Ranch Market
looking for parsley and cabbage at 3 am
I might say a cricket has fallen
and here is another angelic bard
corrupting the populace

I still can't do long division
or file a tax form or understand the stock market
or tie my shoelaces properly, some things
just lay beyond my grasp

78 pale green Porsche
in the garage next door

dragonfly dressed fit to kill
comes zooming along

in the front yard ladybugs
thick grass, shadow
of a bird soaring overhead

who gives a penny royal?
Imagine the insolence of ancient men
Thinking themselves noble and god-like

I know nothing of such things
yet Homer led into maelstroms

Odysseus returns from 19 years wandering
And puts a key to his storeroom door
                Click!
inside is the faithful weapon
patiently waiting, of good use
when he slays those
who usurped his honor
blood flows carnival barkers bleed
and fall useless

my archive is fabulous, all those poems
so many notebooks signed editions
a handful of photographs, ephemera,
why should I complain?
Odysseus bends his bow

"Ghost Writer" collage art by T. MIKE WALKER

ANDY CLAUSEN
GLORIOUS SEX

I was young
I thought good sex, I mean, glorious all out sex
    would save the world
Save not only from devastation of war
    but save the material of the planet
I was young and so was she
We dropped and as dawn broke
    slowly over coyote mountains
        onto the Santa Clara valley
(After experiencing ego dissimulation
    reconstructing our personalities
        with what was revealed
    our son's name Cassidy Allen Jones)
Every siren in San Jose started whining
What else could we think other than
    this is it
This is what we practiced pre-natal under our first
    grade desks to survive
We knew about the A-bomb and the N-bomb
    and the Russians
She got on top
This is how we'd thwart the attack & destruction
    and if it is truly Armageddon
We wouldst die in the noblest position

Huge fog horns in the bay
Gigantic steel hull rising
Horses galloping in the orchards
Fruit fermented, birds slurring their trills
Worms like spaghetti in the meat ball
    composting soil
The moon glistening between
    two smooth Eucalypti
The fecund sperm smell of the redwoods
    of the Santa Cruz in spring
        wafting through the window
        that mirrors the morn's Baroque score
    emanating from springs
        of the marriage mattress
Every ancestor reborn in our blood erupting
DNA candle flicker and pistons pound a rotation
    a rotary goes around comes around
Climax is Anti-Climax
The treasure is in the seeking
    the finding is just all right
There is nothing more pure or clean
Pop goes the weasel, groovin high
    the Bird gets the worm
Bop the fun
Pleasure the bodies unlimited
Heat & sweat unbridled laughter
Eyes illumined jewels
    adorning the carnival skin
We used to plant little flags when we did it outside
No walls, no roof, no clothes, no regrets, no rules
Who needs a motel room
    when we have the top of Mt. Tamalpais

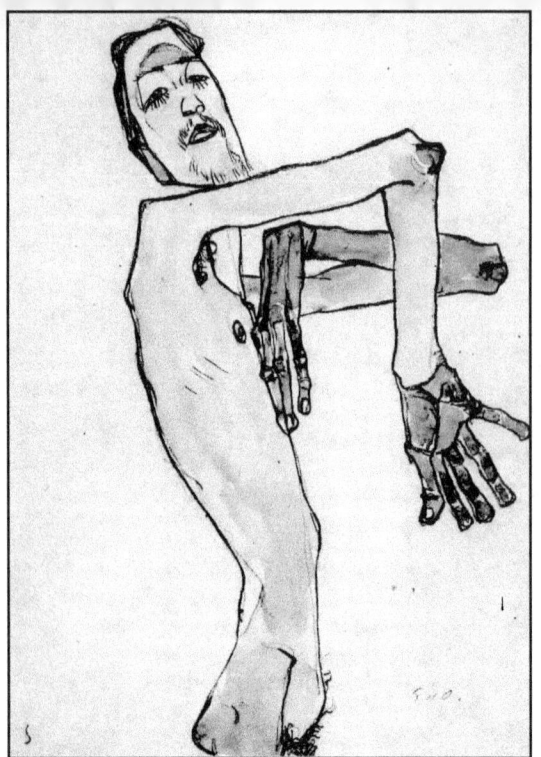

"Mime van Osen with crossed arms" by EGON SCHIELE, 1910

BRENDAN CONSTANTINE
X MARKS THE X

You want to cross your arms,
and by you, I mean you reading this,
you with your good arm

and your ashamed arm. You, who haven't
had enough water today and haven't read
the book you've been meaning to.

You, who crossed your arms as a child
and wondered, *Is it going to stay like this?*
You want to do it again.

This isn't mysterious, not a murder
mystery, except to the extent
that the world is.

And if you regard the world as alive,
if you believe the sky is watching
and the ground is bearing,

then the murder rate for everyone is
a hundred percent. But right now,
we're talking about you,

you who's so God damn lucky because
the killers are distracted and haven't
noticed either of us.

Chances are they'll get me first,
so, I can say the word *You* again
and you can draw this page a little

closer to your face, your elbows
almost touching.

BRENDAN CONSTANTINE
JOKES ABOUT ANGELS

An angel walks into a hospital and says,
*I need to see a doctor. The nurse asks,
What's the matter? and the angel says,
Nothing, I've just never seen one.*

How many angels does it take to change
the subject?

It's midnight and a hospital is burning.
A sperm of helicopters swim above it,
aiming big cones of light so the firemen
can tell the building from the night.
Most of the patients have fled, but many
are missing and presumed transcendent.
A woman in a wheelchair pulls her robe
together. Two doctors share a cigarette
nearby. One says something in Ukrainian.
The other nods in Ukrainian. Soft music
starts playing from a coat pocket. No one
stops watching the flames.

An angel walks into a bar and orders *The usual*.
Everything happens.

ORDELL CORDOVA
FORGOTTEN ANCESTORS

Let's me drop it
To my ancestors
Left and forgotten
Nations and nations
Of forgotten ancestors
Black
Who connected themselves
To Egypt
And
Ethiopia
Hope ya look it up
Even as most history
Is corrupt
Those fake historians
Slip up
Truth slides thru
Here a light
To illuminate
These ancestors
Here I see you

You Dubh, woo, hu, ohh,
Dubh Glas
Murray's and Russells
From the Woo/Hu bird
Nile Valley
Seen
In the Stella of Narmer
Misinterpreted
Scorpion King
This is the forgotten ancestors
Of Europe
Black as Africa
Connected
Seen on

Ancient Crest
From Scotland
I know
You saw u
N Egypt
N Ethiopia
N Africa
Forgotten ancestors

Eye C u
I See u

Eye C u
Gypsies
A mix of many
Many Black peoples
Of ancient

You Dubh, woo, hu, ohh,
Dubh Glas
Murray's and Russells
Nigers
Noir
Swartz
From the Woo/Hu bird
Nile Valley
Seen
From
The Clowns
The Minstrels
Just as
On the Stella
Of Narmer

Forgotten ancestors

Eye C U
I see you
Ancestors
From
Venus of Willendorf
To the Jacobites
Bringing that
Gypsie
Thru Slavery
And Scotch
We always made it
Made it bounce
Our songs
From the Highlands
To the
Sahara
From
Cheddar
To
Gambia
Stonehenges
Opening the door
To your perception
I want u
2 C
2 C
These ancestors
Black and forgotten
By historians
Not by me

Eye C U
I see you
Ancestors
You're not forgotten

"I Heard the News Today, Oh Boy!" art by GEORGE MILO BUCK

CATHYANN CUSIMANO
A PIECE OF TOAST AND THE END OF THE WORLD

The end of the world begins with a piece of toast,
winged eyeliner, breakfast as usual,
star-searching comet streak heralding angel
falling on white noise ears…a piece of wheat toast
spread with jam.

The end of the year begins with
dry, dry, dry, dry, bam!!!
rain, rain, rain, rain float into new,
drag grey cloud Linus-blanket over
countdown of remaining days.

The end of sanity begins with
broken hearts full of diamond dust
joy-relics strewn on particle-board floors,
fragments of the heart, scraps of the mind
blender set to pulverize, meal replacement
thoughts with shrieking silence and
epidemic sound.

The end of anything begins with ordinary,
least expected, can't force it, dust on a
windowsill, a light switch flick to lions in
the room, one minute a piece of toast,
the next, the end of the world.

PAUL CORMAN-ROBERTS
THIS TRAIN HAS BEEN TAKEN OUT OF SERVICE

Bear witness now:

The Captain America
for our generation
sports Heshen ink
on his shaved melon
aims his righteous rage
at the young man
who jams
the commuter car doors open
so as not to miss his ride
around the way
but now the train doors are stuck
because he has done this
and the train
has been taken out of service.

Captain America
drags the young man
the length of the platform
delivers his yelping,
protesting package
of millennial male regret
at the feet
of the Bay Area Rapid Transit's Finest
where they are both faced up
with equal charges
of sabotage and assault
making for a push

In which case Captain America
always wins out
the abstract
which doesn't change the fact
he too,
has been dragged
the length of the platform.

after everything   you call me dark

tonight, I put aside posies and false positivity

Lilith resides in my twelfth house
she unbinds my hair
with patient fingers

and as the moon rises above
the valley of bones

I unleash my dark self

recognize my fading beauty
dance with the music   of time

visit with dead friends
see the snake
swallow
its own tail

see what is rising from the depths

attend to the spiritual, the sexual,
the emotional

enter my second Saturn returns

take out the broom and sweet
release my dragon

with its ravenous appetite to   the part of life
that it touches

drop the question: accept the algorithm   of the universe

anchor yourself and return
to the eternal now

courage can't be tested sluggishly

create a rise in your altar
for pink rose petals,
rosemary, a
crimson candle

dark or light

I am the wind blowing through your house,
your hair, your heart

I own this history

everyone knows who   wrote the book

I am someone
not something

and this: forgiveness is not absolution

JOHN DORSEY
POEM FOR THE NICOLAS CAGE SUPER FAN
AT THE ELLIS FISCHEL CANCER CENTER

we weren't meant
to sit in waiting rooms
in paper masks

but once you make it through the zombie apocalypse
rooms like this are all that's left
a pale young girl
not even old enough to drive
has medical bracelets on up to her elbows
& a single tattoo of a rose
half visible on her upper shoulder

she prays for a fiery car crash
or some light hand to hand combat
while jumping out of a plane
that's running out of gas
that she calls her body
anything exciting enough
to wake her from the stupor
of her medication
as she talks to me about nic cage
for at least ten minutes

maybe this conversation
has been going on for centuries
we all pray to our own gods
vampires & holy men

sometimes you have to let out a scream
in the middle of the night
because it just feels right
shaking the cancer from your skin

sometimes you have to imagine
what nic cage would do in this situation
& i think my god will punch your god right in the face
because sometimes
that feels right too.

"Craig Easley at Sparring With Beatnik Ghosts: Round 2" by Steven C. Wilson.

CRAIG EASLEY
HU-MAN

WHO BOMBED A PEARL
TO START A WAR?

WHO GASSED & OVEN'D
6 MILLION OR MORE?

WHO CLONED THEN SOLD
THE NEW GOLDEN CALF?

WHO'S DENIED EVERY HOLOCAUST
OF HIS BLOODTHIRSTY PAST?

O NO NOT ME MAN,
YES,
YOU MAN!

WHO MANUFACTURED THE KILLING FIELDS
OF SOUTHEAST ASIA?

WHO SLAUGHTERED THE CZAR & HIS FAMILY…
EVEN ANASTASIA?

WHO SPLIT THE ATOM WITH HIS MUSROOM'D VISIONS
OF SKULL & BONES?

WHO CLAIMS HE LONGS FOR PEACE…BUT
JUST CAN'T LEAVE WAR ALONE?

WHO BUILT HIS HOUSE HOLY
IN THE MIDDLE EAST?

WHO'S TURNED THE GARDEN OF EDEN
INTO A BLOOD HUNGRY BEAST?

O NOT ME MAN,
YES,
YOU MAN

NO YOU MUST MEAN
FU-MAN-CHU
MAN,

NO
I MEAN HU-
MAN!

the old ponzi

ANA ELSNER
THE DAY OF THE PARADE

It was on the Day of the Parade
when the emperor's marching band played off-key,
stripped down to their skivvies,
at gunpoint.

What else could one do when there was no else.

I was swinging from the trapeze,
and you tossed your boyish laughter up at me,
and I caught it in my cupped hand
while not letting go.

Any hobnobber can tell that you and I
were cut from the same wrought cloth.
But the apprentice has to look dangerously close,
to figure out that you and I
did not bleach and shrink together in one wash.
It took so many rinse cycles for me to come clean,
while you collected the sanitized dividends
from a good pre-soaking.

On the night you faded to grey,
superstition came raining down on my head,
and I could not wash it out of my hair
for a long time.

But after the official body count,
I divorced the Black-Cat crowd
and tasted the mint julep tide,
lapping at my tongue,
which longed only for your mouth.

Then there were the riots in the streets,
and all these awful mac-'n-cheese dinners;
And every humdrum night,
the hired dreams
and the unholy anticipation.

And when you finally got off the plane,
and arrived at the point,

where you had enough of all the shilly-shallying,
customs was already closed for the night.

But you had nothing to declare anyway,
except for your shame,
which is duty-free,
at least for now.

You made appear on my bitterling bed
glaciers of chocolate,
of complicity
and your pungent scent.

And nothing remains undone
as I circumnavigate
the slopes and plains
of your streamlined body
with my nostrils quivering.

That night, we fell just one kiss short.

ALEXIS RHONE FANCHER
DON'T WASH

*"I'm returning in three days. Don't wash."**

I touch myself so I can savvy what you rut in. Bring my fingers to my mouth, imagine you in our bed, returned from the three-day fray, redolent of the weight of the world, and me, your dirty, dirty girl, naked, eager, as you make your way down, breathing in my hair, my lips, the sweet spot where neck meets collarbone. I've made a religion of your fantasies, a science of what you desire. That ferine moan, my always startled gasp at first thrust. I angle, cocked hips, a bit askew. How I arch for maximum penetration, hands pushing against your chest, while my thighs pull you in. Our bed is a rocket launch, a bacchanal, a pelican's steep dive into the sea. I revel in that you revel in me. A lifetime away from Michael, my first love, that long ago when I'd used the freshening wipe before I arrived, so as not to offend. I'd spread myself wide on his bed, confident, watching the top of his head (black curls) as he explored me — that fear of not being Summer's Eve™ fresh, worried my pussy might disenchant, the musk of me — all wiped away. He raised his head. *Next time,* Michael said, once he'd tasted me. *Don't wash.*

*From a love letter Napoleon sent to Josephine

Published in SWWIM, Summer, 2020

*Art by **JERRY KAMSTRA** — from the Kamstra Sparchive Collection.*

The sirens have been
screaming lies about us;

those emergencies proclaiming
we're their bastard next of kin,
children of oblivion and broken glass;

worried wanderers
roaming pitiless cities
of demolished optimism;

our cold bones clattering
like a failed fortune teller's
shuffled deck of cards—

paralyzed predictions,
doom-age daydreams;

wounds unwound into paths
where we're crossed
and double-crossed
by black cats
engaged in hex trafficking.

The sirens
have been screaming lies about us;

claiming we've got bulletholes for eyes,
that our mind's white space
has been filled with suicide notes
scribbled in misery's ink;

that our every moment is spent
taping up the busted windows of shattered souls;

that our names
have adopted all the aliases of pain;

that we're ravenous and raving
as a lunatic's tied-off vein,
craving a syringe of serenity
that'll never come.

Sirens wail a ballad shambles,
sirens make the word *flower*
sound like *murder*,
sirens unsheathe their knives,
slash the night with death cries.

The sirens
have been screaming lies about us;

that we're pimps and pariahs,
monotone messiahs
decked out in sallow-skinned promises
of raptureless tomorrows;

that our remaining graces
cross-dress as annihilating angels;

that our scraps of good intentions
have been ravaged by mind traps,
kill cults, and outlaw death trips.

The sirens say
we've got the keys
to the extinction machine;

that we've landed a major role
in Dante's *Inferno*;

that we're haters, hedonists,
and heart arsonists
whose stuffed-down angers
are dry weeds in fire season,
begging for a match.

Sirens wail a ballad shambles,
sirens make the word *flower*
sound like *murder*,
sirens unsheathe their knives,
slash the night with death cries.

The sirens
have been screaming lies about us;

that deep within our chests
are burlap sacks
packed with rabid dogs
craving the raw meat of gutterspeak
and bloodclot lullabies;

dogs howling, growling, foaming at the mouth,
temperaments built
from lost bets and the short end
of broken wishbones.

The sirens say
our inner weather
is thunderstorms
followed by swarms of torment;

that we're incurable cretins
tearing down Xanax edens,
that grief's got us on speed dial,
that our fantasies
got a date with the coroner down on the street

Sirens wail a ballad shambles,
sirens make the word *flower*
sound like *murder*,
sirens unsheathe their knives,
slash the night with death cries.

Some nights
those sirens are so loud
only tombstones
can sleep through it all.

JACK FOLEY
THE MARX BROTHERS RUN THE COUNTRY

Foist-a we gonna t'row out da economy
Who's-a need da economy,
Says Chico
Yes, I do remember we had an economy
Says Groucho. Say, who let this fellow in here?
(Harpo: …)
Den-a we gonna t'row out da army
We don't-a need da army
We nice-a fellas we give-a da army to da Arabs
Dat a way we get rid-a da terrorism
If they gotta da army they no need da terrorism
They can attack us fair and square
Makes sense to me, says Groucho
(Harpo: …)
Den-a dere's-a da politicians—
Hey I'm a politician, says Groucho
You a politician? asks Chico
Well yes, says Groucho, I'm Senator Hugo Z. Hackenbush
Oh, says Chico, I'm a no recognize you
You da Hack in the Bush
Or da Bush in da Hack
Dat's-a some joke huh boss?
Da Bush is a hack
I'm-a gonna tell-a you what
I like-a you I'm gonna give-a you Delaware
Well, that's mighty White of you, says Groucho
Sho, I'm a good-a guy
You can-a wreck Delaware
(Harpo: …)
But you no can-a wreck da rest o da country
I'm a gonna give-a dat to him
(Harpo smiles)
I'm a gonna give-a him da bomb
(Harpo smiles)
and-a poisonous emissions
(Harpo smiles)
and plenty money
(Harpo smiles)
Den he can-a ruin everybody
Hey, says Groucho, you can't do that
Why not? says Chico
Because you're Italian
Everybody knows Italians don't have any power except in New York City
(Harpo frowns)
And besides, you need to be a lawyer to be president
I need-a a liar? asks Chico
You sure do, says Groucho, and I tell you I'm your man
(Harpo pulls out an American flag and waves it)
I'm the biggest liar you ever met
And I'm gonna make the whole world miserable

The Marx Brothers.

CONTINUED NEXT PAGE

(Harpo pulls out a trumpet and blows it soundlessly)
Armageddon here we come
That's a sound a good a to me, says Chico
Hey whadda you say you name is?
Hugo Z. Hackenbush, says Groucho
Dat's a too long, says Chico
We gotta da short attention span
Nobody's gonna remember dat
How's about we shorten-a da name
Ok, says Groucho. What shall we make it?
How's-a about **BUSH**
Sounds good to me!
We gonna make-a lots a money
(Harpo pulls out a dollar bill from his coat and waves it)
We gonna make-a war not-a love
(Harpo pulls out a sign that says DON'T GET LAID / INVADE)
We gonna be a fine bunch of comedians, dat's a right
(Harpo silently laughs and laughs)
But wait a minute-a, says Chico, observing Harpo
He's-a laugh but he's-a make-a no sound
Maybe he's a cryin
(Harpo sheds a tear)
Maybe he's a no happy about what-a we doin
(Harpo begins to weep copiously)
You know, says Groucho, I'm not so happy about what we're doing either
(Groucho begins to weep)
Dats-a strange, says Chico, we da funniest guys dat ever lived
And nobody's a laugh, everybody's a sad
Everybody's a weep
(Chico begins to sob too)
You bet your life says Groucho
And you know, he says, lying down on the floor, I think you lost the bet
(Groucho begins to moan)
I'm a think we all lost, says Chico
Even the duck is dead, says Groucho
As it drops from the sky and falls on his head
They all lie down on the floor and weep
Harpo pulls out a Black Flag from his coat and waves it above their bodies
They are
Silent

*A middle 1980s trio named themselves **minutemen** for the reason that all their initial originals were designed to last only 60 seconds, plus there was. always, that American Revolution vibe. It must be pointed out that there are not many bands so inclined to invite a poet to compose lines to be transcribed and placed on the 1ˢᵗ page of their record company press kit. In the gutless mindless apathetic world of 21ˢᵗ Century music, it would never happen. Again: however, George Hurley, D Boone and Mike Watt were in a class, totally, by themselves. This late 20ᵗʰ-Century set of lines follows:*

MICHAEL C FORD
MINUTEMEN

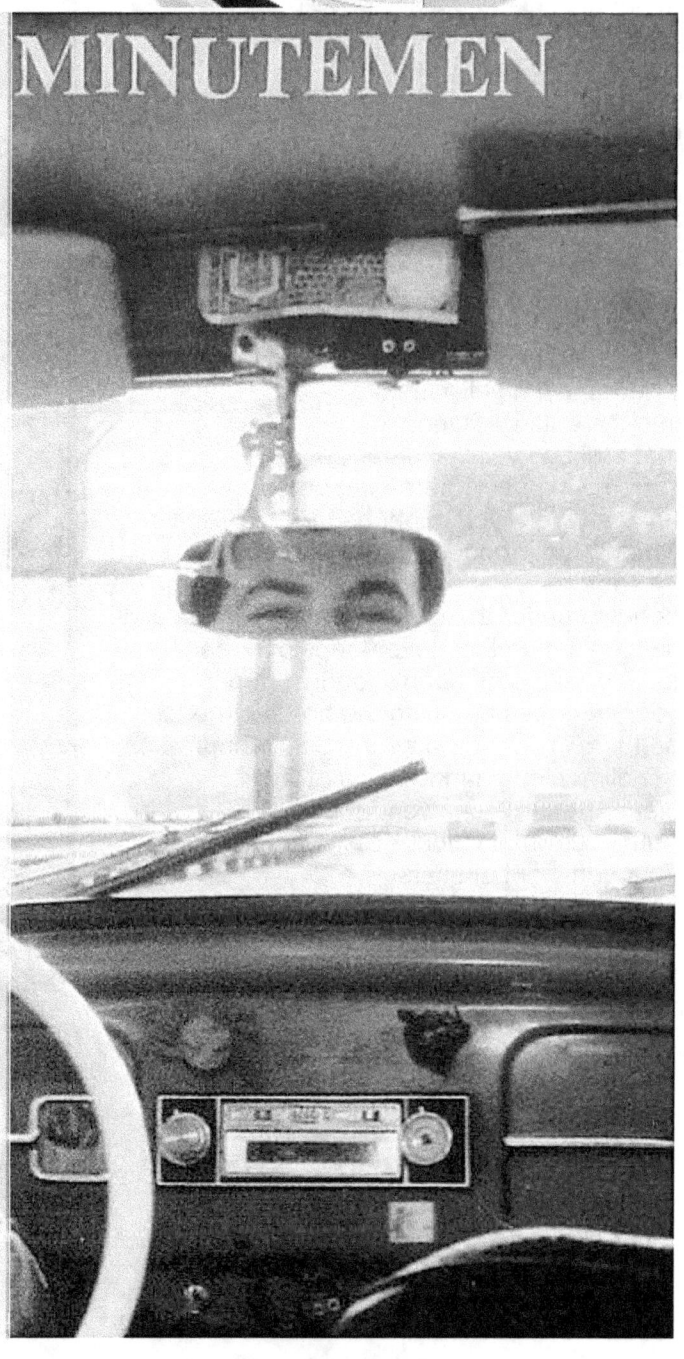

We'll give you just one minute to come outa there with your hands up, all of you singer/song-writer rhymers. We gotcha covered, you disco dippies, you pop-music parasites. Come out fast with

your platinum competition hustles. We got the goods on your gang of greed mongering gargoyles and we're gonna watch you slide down the grease of your own misguided egos and pseudo-journalistic

sabotage. We showed up to save the rancher's daughter. We wanna take back all that formulaic hack-trash and supermarket surrealism and sophomoric stupid sewage you sold her for a

million dollars. We'd like to watch you careerist opportunist literary politicians sink into an academic cesspool. Why don't you poet-tasting twits cancel your subscriptions to the

periodical poetry rags you worship as bibles in your government-funded seminars. You're under arrest, you computer-kissing, system-sucking vermin. You will all be reincarnated as wretches of the wasteland. Some of you will inhabit a polluted PhD swamp in disguise to keep from being lynched. This is your last warning. Okay, boys, let's go in and get 'em.

Irvine, [KUCI-FM] California *(1986)*

DOUBLE NICKELS ON THE DIME

AMÉLIE FRANK
THE PRAIRIE LOVERS

Because, in the end,
you fell for the poet woman
herself enduring and lonesome on the prairie
herself unable to name the stars,
penning verse furiously
as if the drying inkwell were
the great reservoir of her ideas
penning until the big sky gave out,
gave way to more nameless bodies
she, drying her bright eyes,
weaving her words with faded hat ribbon
into the nettleworks of tumbleweeds,
weaving praises of limber, bistred hares,
dashing between rosa arkansana
and patches of bluestem
weaving with fingers that lost their luster
to honest work eons ago
then casting the homely, thorny vessels
into the pass of cedars
where they might bound
into the cutting Chinooks
that crossed your own barren trail,
you, cutting back, gathering verse,
unsure where you might bed for the season,
whether your bones could still take the ground
if needs be,
bedding under the nameless, glittering bodies,
holding fast to the clever loops of ribbon
as you read a girlhood's fondest hopes,
your fingertips brushing the barbs of her call
bedding in your dreams the poet woman,
her climacteric hands again at work,
dispelling the atonic, enduring ache
from your hands, your head,
your continent of scars
her silvery eyes patiently
seeking out the nameless above,
awaiting the response of the nameless.

"The Gathering" collage art by T. MIKE WALKER.

BEA GARTH
ON WHAT IS REQUIRED

I wintered far too long
thick roots strangled my every movement
as I dreamed of Spring
despite what seemed all odds
willing myself to un-twine
the hidden spells that bound me.

Miraculously, I woke up
knowing what finally to do:
what majicks to enact, what potions to drink,
what edibles to eat, what things to avoid.

Slowly I revive
as I finally begin to turn the soil
and spread the rich compost

that sat forgotten
through that dark forbidding Winter.

Now I hear the Earth Sprites laugh
waiting for the new starts:
tomato, yellow-squash, cucumber,
rosemary, thyme, sage and rue,
brilliant red marigold
and its cousin -- golden calendula.

And, despite the lateness of Spring,
the earliness of Summer
grabs me by my hands
during this pregnant New Moon,
showing me Winter truly has passed
and will not come again for some Time
but Action Now is of the Essence.

NELSON GARY
BLANK FRANK

Behind the wheel of his blue 1952 Studebaker Starlight coupe, Frank Lee's wounded, serpentine intestines clenched as he took the turn onto Main Street. The blank's penetrating blast hurt *like hell—ha, a cliché—death, another cliché.* If he could have shat the anguish out, he would have, but that was no more than a fool's dream as the blood rushed from his grimace with a series of groans. The threat of death can make anyone a fool, a dreamer, or both. Everything, for the driver, was faint now as the blood saturated his blue and gold flannel with sanguine darkness. This situation could turn into his death in under an hour, and, of course, the apple-red life force drenched his green Dickies— noir Christmas. His life didn't speed before his eyes as he looked for somewhere to park; he'd taken more than a few shots in the past (for far better reasons from far better people). In the passenger seat, ruddy-faced Adam Lawson's piece had gone off in his hand, firing a blank. "Was it an accident, Adam?"

"Hell yes! Something's wrong with this fuckin' gun. It's a blank, Frank. We were just going to scare the shit out of these guys with nothin' but a big noise."

"At close range, nothin' can kill you."

"Nothing?!"

"Nothing, a blank. You should know that. You should know a lot of things you don't seem to. Ah, fuck! I've known for a long time you're hiding shit, Adam." Frank looked Lawson in the eye, one quick glance. He parked the car against an elm tree. Feeling as if his guts were going to fall out onto his shoes, the gas, and the brakes, Lee rested his arm against his bloody stomach, dropped his head to the wheel, then turned his face a tad toward short-haired Lawson. Frank rolled his eyes at Adam. "I have the world to say to you, man, but I don't think it's worth it at this juncture."

"I understand."

"You understand nothing," Frank's stated, then grunted, holding back a groan. "Actually, you don't understand even that—nothin'! If you understood that, you'd understand this." Frank reached into his pants' pocket, removed his Glock 19, and blew Adam the mole's brains out.

SPENCER GRIFFIN
UNCLE BILLY

Uncle Billy! He's so silly!
His house is made of chocolate cake
Everything in his house is alive
Even the walls talk, for goodness' sake!
Uncle Billy! He's so silly!
Has a burger for a pet
He takes him for walks 'round the neighborhood
And feeds him well so he's not upset
He wears his shoes upon his head
And keeps his hat under his feet
And after a dinner of ice cream sundaes,
Vegetables are his special treat
After a long day of doing nothing,
Uncle Billy says goodnight
Tucks himself in bed with his feet on his pillow,
Opens his eyes, and turns on the light.

S.A. GRIFFIN
KOWALSKI
for Barry Newman (1930–2023)

Barry Newman has left the building
but lives on as cinematic anti-hero
Kowalski, built for speed
tearing up the road behind the wheel of his ghostly white
1970 Dodge Challenger R/T 440 Magnum in *Vanishing Point*
Mile High to Golden Gate in 15 hours
in an all bets are off game of
you bet your life

Cleavon Little as blind D.J. Super Soul
the divine Virgil with an ear to the police band
sightless seer guiding Kowalski thru the inferno
of Vietnam era America

Kowalski nailed to the cross tops
buzzing to the desert radio
grieving the loss of a love burning inside out
decorated vet on the run from bad cops
and the horror of a war that nobody wanted

in time you would work the other side of the law
on the small screen as *Petrocelli* receiving
well-earned Emmy and Golden Globe nods

but you will always be the lone driver
blazing blue highways beyond borders
where Kowalski lives!
too damn fast for the law
too damn cool for the heat
too big a heart for this small world
as the camera pans
a dog barks
a siren wails
and it is Sunday morning in America

and this poem is named *Kowalski*
first, last and only
for Barry Newman as the last American hero
smiling into the lens
vaporizing into the *molecule of speed*
the vanishing point
where sooner or later we all meet
where all good stories begin
at the end

– S.A. Griffin
6/13/23

JONATHAN HARRIS
BUKOWSKI GOES PUBLIC WITH HIS FIRST REVELATION

I knew
by the end of
grade 7
I wouldn't be
popping into the Y
for years
when voted
Most Adorable.

"Dali" drawing in stone by JOE FUNK (Venice, CA, 1968). Fron the Kamstra Sparchive Collection.

JONATHAN HARRIS
SEX WITH SALVADOR DALI

He drinks in
  with his eyes,
makes out
  with his ears,
draws breath
  with his nose,
blows smoke
  with his mouth.
Besides being
  surreal, it's over
before it started
  & hard to grasp.

The little prick.

JONATHAN HARRIS
PLAYING WITH FIRE

Little heads poke out of a matchbox
sitting on top of big head's
blank pad of paper who,
beside them in a chair,
keeps one eye on the clock
& the other on the door
open to the outside world
waiting, as all poets will,
penniless loafers
tapping on the floor,
for lightning to strike
& whatsherface the Muse
to blow in on the draft.

ELYSE HART
NORTHWARD REGRESSION

Leaving now for the black cottonwood,
Sitka spruce speckling a city so green.
Take your executorship
and POAs and health directives,
give them to the other daughter
    the one that doesn't exist.
Can you float alone?
    I'd like to rub a rubber sole into soil so clean.

Let me go where everyone is
heading into another decade of
life—sparkling and rosy!
And I'm a passenger,
and time is not round.
    I'd like to see a tree that's not a palm.
Can I float alone?

My eyes are shriveling—
we are in a desert that ends at the sea.
    This is where my calcium blows.
Every memory will settle
in a mussel shell that lives there
on the pier pilings.

ELYSE HART
CAUGHT IN A PALM

A smirk is the distance
from when I last fell and rolled in grass
and when I wanted to be cupped
    but ripped
seam to seam
like I'd been cut from felt
    and stitched with a leather lace,

inside me the cries of strangers
who had ceased to be strangers
    but not their strangeness—
had wanted to be mothers
or fathers or actor or reapers,

slipping their token of emptiness
    through a hole
where was without selvage
or sword or words to say
    keep away, to yourself, be gone!

let me float on my isle of pins,
my tuft of unwoven threads
    caught in a palm.

MICHAEL LAYNE HEATH
THE FINAL TESTAMENT OF CHARLIE NOTHING

If all the maidens grieve a death
that will excuse the imprints of life
Who'll stamp my papers of mistaken identity
At the final border for which I strive?

Where across the plaza is convened a sentence
that will be debated for years
how will be divined my infinite longing
and staunch these obstinate tears?

When romance loses pace of its judicious taste
like a barfly at quarter to two
And the latest young beard with a parlance spat weird
Makes for expressions threatening to you.

I never play cards so trips to Reno are hard
With no cowboys or drag queens around
So just give me cruel fingernails on strings
And an honest blare of sunshine in sound.

Where muffled Rota trumpets queue
along with rampant seagull guitars
joining K.C. stride and Sturgis ultra-glide
boarding Sun Ra's ninth rocket to the stars.

E PENNIMAN JAMES
THE KAUFBOMB

In mitigated circumstance
You chose erasure
And silenced
Your ohsosingular voice
Master abombunist
Glorifier of oatmeal cookies
You spent your second April
Counting the holes
In Kennedy's head
Bayou boatman
Submachine marine
Dragging the bale
Beyond the pale
In heavy water
Wandering the alleyways of Chinatown
North Beach
Emperor of the existential bagel
Declaiming gone visions
Atop the tables
Of forgotten coffeeshops
Gathering leaves
And scraps of loveliness
To be torn asunder
By the madness
Of America

JIMMY JAZZ
HELPER

A man in a wheelchair
hailed one of my students

Can you hold this cup for me son?

It was a waxy paper cup from 7/11

He did

My student felt the warmth
looking at it, curiously, not knowing the word 'urine,' thinking in images, groping for language

the amygdala switches the senses on

Suddenly, you see a bottle at the curb, you notice the trash strewn all around, spilled food, flies,
soiled rags

A siren, ambulance, echoes down the block

The acrid smell comes on like two shots of tequila,
the dry wet smell pushes into his nose
as it crawls up into his mind

Mudbricks itself in like

your first kiss
your first corpse
your first failure

He saw the man's feet swollen, a chiaroscuro of scabbed & open sores

He saw then the man's pants gathered low on the sidewalk
He saw the black hairs, the ugly dick
the dribbled wet spot

Can you help me pull up my pants?

He did

My student pulled this man's pants up around his hips

That was very kind of you, I said. You should always help if you can, but next time, be more careful
He could've had a needle in his pocket. You could have gotten poked

I saw in his face that there wouldn't be a next a time
that even the most charitable among us have limits

I saw a naïveté dissolve
            a butterfly snatched by a mockingbird mid-flight

This wouldn't happen in my country, he said
We take care of people, we have hospitals

Most people here, I said, say people should take of care of themselves

GARY JUSTICE
THIS IS NOT DADA

Thus misspoke
my Zarathustra
miss-treatise
alphabetic soup
dynamic pantomime
Shakespeare on a stick
trick my treat
doublespeak
drip drop hip hop
sylababble scrabble
scryptic riddles
non-sense-sequitur
whiskey and rhyme
just for the rum of it
assault and lime
verbs and spice
paradise …paradigm

© Gary Justice, 8/2/13

"Keiko's Dream" art by BEA GARTH.

JAMES EVERT JONES
RIVALRY

six feet beneath Westwood
awkward as fuck
these manly men measure
their worm-eaten dicks
to gain her favor
to turn her glance
their way

whose turn is it?
does she sidle up
to the baseball jersey
or the silk PJ's?
the ever-present pipe
or the bottomless
coffee-maker?
Is she a day person
or a party girl
even now?

and if she were
to change her mind
how long
would it take for her
to look the other way?

or maybe they're
simply happy
as an eternal threesome?

Art by JERRY KAMSTRA — from the Kamstra Sparchive Collection.

JERRY KAMSTRA
HEY, I KNOW RICHARD BRAUTIGAN

(Excerpt from Kamstra's book *Big Sur and the Sour Grapes of Henry Miller*)

"Hey, I know Richard Brautigan. How long has he been down here?"

"Three months. He's with a character named Price Dunn. A real rebel."

A year and a half later (1961) I would be living in Big Sur in Limekiln Canyon and Price Dunn would become my neighbor, the lead character of Brautigan's Confederate General From Big Sur, yes, this was the Confederate General, moving in here now, actually into an abandoned house high up onna cliffside overlooking the canyon, with his battered pickup and lady from Canada, ex-wife of poet Irving Layton, with her beautiful 9 year old daughter Naomi, moving into Limekiln Canyon into idyllic pre-rules Edenlike setting that we'd been enjoying for the past four months, we being me and Pat Cassidy & his girl Betty, & Kentucky, a kid who showed up one day from Kentucky and so that was his name, reddish bearded fine young fellow filled with innocence and grace, all of us working on the Big Sur bridges which they were replacing, all the old redwood bridges coming down and being replaced with concrete trusses (this due to 50's cold war paranoia for possible need for heavy military equipment to move along coast road, redwood bridges can't carry heavy Abrams tanks!), and we were in there mixing the mud, camping out in Limekiln Canyon at night, Cassidy havin' built up a small hut-like cabin out of scrap plywood from the construction site, and Kentucky himself hand building his wee domicile from old timbers and boards and saplings, and me simplifying my life by sleeping outside unner the stars inna bag onna ground, simplicity itself, tho at evening goin' over t'Cassidy's really quite impressive hut and hanging around the cookstove, his gal Betty with him then, and this actually being the beginning of my real career in Big Sur, sending later for a gurl myself, Lesley, who would later be my first wife and the mother of my first two children, Duke and Miakje.

Looking back down the road Frances was pointing out, where Richard Brautigan the incipient poet and Price Dunn the Done-in general were staying, I did not know what future lay in store for me as far as Big Sur or these two characters were concerned, that we'd become good friends, both Richard and I incipient authors at this time, even visiting together later in North Beach studios talking about how we would be famous together, everyone quite surprised when Richard did become famous, and even more surprised when he killed himself. What I also did not know was that Bob,

CONTINUED NEXT PAGE

the husband I was about to meet, would later take his own life in some insanity deceptions while in jail in San Luis Obispo, San Louie they call it, or Slomo, said nickname announcing the pace of the place, pretty slow when you're dead, in a cell for stabbing to death a sailor on a bus due to insanity paranoias while returning up the coast to Gorda, Bob an ex-G.I back from Korea where he prolly had some problems, simple ones like killing your so-called government-appointed enemies, and now taking his own life. These preludes too to the fact that the very land we were now driving on was, according to Frances, owned by a crazy lady and her crazy son, Madelaine Boyd and Pat, renowned for nuttiness, a wild woman up onna hill here who sold a bit of her precious land to Bob and Frances, 60 acres, money needed to pay taxes, and that land down below across the road wherein dwelled Brautigan and Price Dunn and a host of frogs if you remember, that piece is also owned by this strange eccentric let's not call her crazy lady. And disputes and battles were going on about land hereabouts. And rocks were falling. And Richard Brautigan was hitting his head on that low ceiling Price built. And then he shot himself. What can you expect in this hazy world?

"Hey, I Know Richard Brautigan" is an excerpt from the upcoming book BIG SUR AND THE SOUR GRAPES OF HENRY MILLER by Jerry Kamstra (book cover art by FITZ).

Opposite page: "Bixby Canyon" art by JERRY KAMSTRA — from the Kamstra Sparchive Collection.

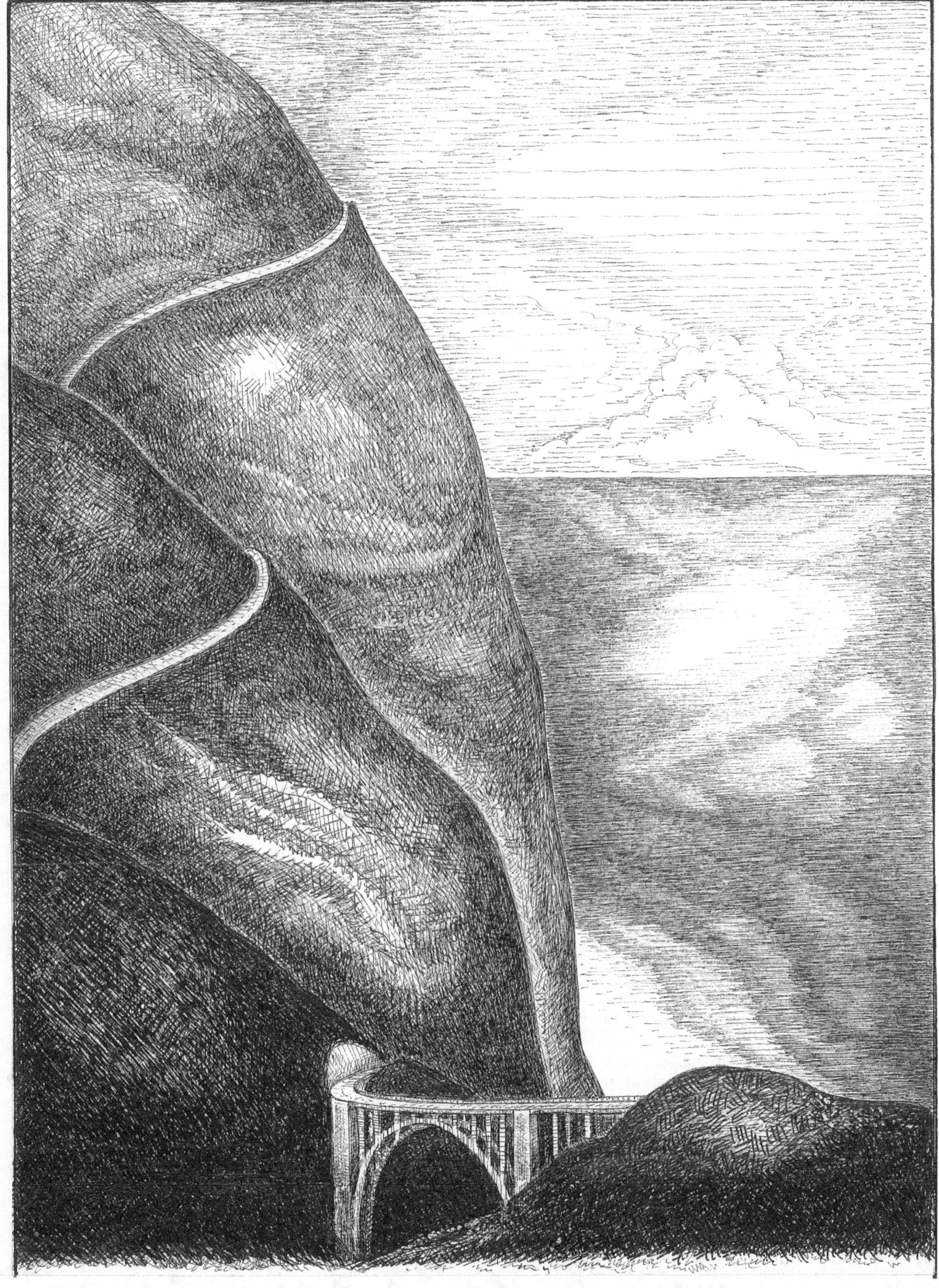

KAREN KAPLAN
TRANSITION SANTA CRUZ

I dream of a world with water we can drink
Where there is space to think
Where men could wear pink
No one wears mink
And we're not on the brink.

I dream of a time when everything is fine
No one dines on a sacred bovine.

I dream of a place where there's plenty to eat
We hear the same beat
And we share the same heat.

We give and receive
Community weaves
The energy of life
A world without strife.

Transitioning back to nature again
I bake quiche with eggs from my hen
And share organic fruit from my garden
Whatever I give comes back multiplied by ten
I write poetry with a pen
G-d, Buddha, Allah Amen!

ROYAL KENT
POETS RIFF

from the soul bearing falsettos of an eddy kendricks
or a phillip bailey

the resonance of the bass I'm thinking jack Jamison
or esperanza Spaulding

bringing crescendos like the wind
macoy tynors jazz riffs that ascend
and descend according to the plan of
some mystifying physics defying all logic

plucked from the strings of the
avant garde pianist joe zawinul
with the adderlys nat & cannonball
takin a stand
the drama of dramatics
the chi lites bringing spoken word and song
stylistics stylin

the mystics of the word
dylanistic smokey poetry
holland dozier holland
rhymin the love with heartbreak

sophisticated flare with hendrix swagger
dedicated and honored
understated greatness

setting the landscape of listening
on fire
stirring hearts of desire

when all is said and done
let us give the poets some
spoken word in a form
meant to be heard

On all platforms

Copyright 2023 Royal Kent Edwards

Photo of Royal Kent by DANIEL YARYAN.

JOE KIDD
COMPARED TO WHAT

The air is heavy in our burning lungs.
We have incinerated our candles through a bitter cold night.
The fire throws shadows on a crumbling wall
while artists paint graffiti of ravenous redheads.
Assassins drink wine while their horses take a piss
in a river that has not moved since the age of bronze.
Hunters gather on the southern border
while the light skinned dancers hold babies in arms.
We hear words in conversation that have no origin
as charismatic lawyers fall upon our encampments.
Half of the world now sinks below the surface.
Advanced weapons dig in along imaginary lines.
A flag goes up to end the game of cannibals.

Do not compare:
The light to the darkness
The heat to the cold
The sweetness to the bitterness
The bronze to the gold
The past to the present
The calm to the chaos
The fire to the river
The dancer to the soldier

We live in the city and in the sky
We surf in the desert and the mountain range
It is ours, it is real
In our mind, in our pocket
Causing the birth and the death
and the lives of millions

We are lost
We are alone
We are forever free

JOE KIDD
GARGOYLE STREET

These are the times of exodus from all that lived inside this burned-out ocean, of that line of thought, that lined, patterned, child of neglect called thought. Nothing lives there. Nothing breathes. No expanding and contracting lungs now create a wheezing sound of protest against the emptiness, hollowness, void of what might have been, but won't be.

The army of gods (god's army) surrounded us on the street corner. We threw our knives into the ground below us, stainless steel were the tips of our tongues, fingers, wings, knives in the flesh even though outnumbered, the approaching warriors carried their torches, fueled by hate and human waste product.

Speechless, nothing to say, the poets became normal, boring, repetitive, trying to recapture the runaway slave, the muse, the other that did the work for them as they sat staring. No music could save them now from the silence, also known as certain death.

I, yes, I, sat there watching as the gargoyles climbed the wall. All the way to heaven's angel hole. Their destiny was to guard the yard, like dogs, they were as frightened as the adversaries storming the gate from the inside. So now it was my turn to live forever, to finally get paid the big money that goes with salvation, that goes without saying.

Spent two lifetimes running from the past, but there was no place to go. No platform upon which to stand still, to rest, to catch the heat of a breath in a plastic lung. The machine. The axle upon which the wheel turns the water into blood, into rain. And, the storms raged internal, forever. Laying corpses, one upon another, painful smiles of observers with crooked faces.

Just kick 'em out of the way. You've got something important to do, to write. You gotta move some paper, some bodies, some dirt. We travel light up here. No traffic laws, no lactose, no wires to short. Just wishbones, you know, the long half, the one you never got back home. And, you know what else? You'll never get back home. Period.

So, what have we learned? They are all dead. The dreams. They were not real. Just like you, me, these words, they're not real. It never happened. You never happened. You will understand it someday, everybody does.
That's what eternity is man, all the things that never happened.

RON KOLM
SIZE MATTERS

When I first moved to the Big Apple
I lived in Hell's Kitchen.
I stopped by the Gotham Book Mart
and because I was broke
I asked if they were hiring.
"Sure," a manager replied, pointing
to a small table with a typewriter
surrounded by tall stacks of books.
There was a tiny steel chair
almost hidden beneath it.
"If you can fit, you got the job."
I couldn't and didn't. Luckily the Strand,
a much larger store, eventually hired me
so I was able to remain a New Yorker.

RON KOLM
PENIS ENVY

Penis envy didn't start
With Trump and Putin.
Unfortunately
It goes all the way back
To the dawn of man.
Two males in a cave
Armed with clubs
Circle each other.
"Mine's bigger," one growls.
"No, mine is!" hisses the other.
And then the bashing begins
Until only one primate
Remains standing,
One hand gripping his bloody club
The other cupping his nuts.
He almost seems to smile
As he leaves to find some women
To yell at and push around.

RON KOLM
PENIS EXTENSIONS

Warfare has always been
About extending your will
Further than your enemies.
Stones, spears and bows and arrows
Were all used in fornication.
Then crossbows, muskets,
Cannons and bombs were invented
To fuck with the masses
Until the big one
Finally comes on the scene.
Nuclear weapons are the biggest dicks yet
So we have to keep a watchful eye
On all the tiny fools
Masturbating near the buttons.

LALO KIKIRIKI
THE BUKOWSKI TOUR

Okay, I confess
I took the Bukowski Tour
paid $58 to bus
in the steps
of the master…

We hit the downtown post office first –
Bukowski sorted mail on the third floor –
but I knew the building already
from three days as an extra on Dear God.
Jack Sheldon picked up his trumpet
at one of the counters:
we both made
the final cut;
so I'm thinking,
This stop is on the lalo kikiriki tour, too.

We get back on the bus,
Sunset to Alvarado;
our guide points out some bars:
Short Stop, Gold Room (been there, too)
and we stop at a bungalow court
in Hollywood
where we learn about
Black Sparrow Press,
the monthly stipend and
we all get jealous…

Then up stepped my poetry friend Sina,
from the 90s
who manages the apartment house
next door,
where the Barnsdall Poets met
once or twice.
It has a classy lobby; Sina had cats
but her rooms were immaculate
(also free).
Fifteen years later, she's still there,
still managing,
still beautiful, long red hair.
She wants to sell an autographed
Bukowski paperback - no takers –
most of us had paid nearly
our last dimes
to take the Bukowski tour.

Some are saving for beer
at the next stop;
so we're back on the bus,
up Western to the Pink Elephant

and Baskin Robbins still there, familiar
from my daily walks with baby Charlie
to Griffith Park.

The tour bus parks at the curb
and we all eat free donuts
out of pink boxes
while everyone takes pictures
and some buy beer
in honor of Bukowski.

This stop could have been
on the lalo kikiriki tour
just as easily,
"Every day from April,1980
to September, 1981
lalo pushed the infant Charlie
to Ferndale and back
in a Graco stroller from Zody's on Sunset"
while Bukowski stewed in his juices
on Carlton Way.

The Bukowski Tour, is, it turns out,
too much like
the story of my life,
except for the notorious
alcoholic haze…

Oh, to be Bukowski;
angry,
irresponsible,
careless,
cool
typing relentlessly,
gloriously drunk,
around the corner
from that crazy intersection
Hollywood and Western…
The crime scene taped motel
where shootouts left
bloodstains on the sidewalk
and pimps grabbed high-heeled whores
by their hair,
under the giant hot dog…
we were there
in the thick of it all, unknowing.
Yeah, Bukowski…

The tourists are back on the bus again,
heading down Sunset, the route

taking as long as it took the Minnow
to get around the bay;
those folks never got back
from their three-hour tour.
But we do –
pull up in front of Philippe's,
file out of the bus –
maybe a turkey dip or custard pie
before we slide back into
our own
drab lives,

And we are all
feeling a little gamier,
up for the Gold Room
on the way back to Silver Lake?
reveling in vicarious
degeneracy…
Bukowski always made it look
so easy.

Marc Kockinos at Sparring Round 11 — photo by ELLA SENERES.

MARC KOCKINOS

FAMILIAR EXILE

We wander like refugee's -
under these towers
bleached bone-white by the Sun.

Involuntary exile
down familiar streets,
holding on to the fading images
of all the places
where we'd rather be.

We gather in basement cafe's
and after-hours' clubs,
just outside the easy glamour
and forced enthusiasm
of the Mating game..

We recognize each other
by the searchlight glare's
coming from dark corner tables.
Making eye contact
in an attempt to look deeper
than the carefully applied make-up
and all the cute little gestures
designed to show that *here*
is something exceptional-
look no further..

And they always turn away-
And they always turn away from our gaze
knowing that the rules have changed:
that we could care less
about how cool we look,
and small-talk ain't nothing

but a Band-Aid to cover
the emptiness that hangs thicker
than cigarette smoke in the air.

So I shake hands all around
and nod to an unfamiliar face or two.
Settling deep into a chair
that provides more
of the comforts of home
than the room that I fall asleep in each night.
Where all the memories of childhood
are still engraved into cold stucco walls.

We talk, drink and smoke
into the early morning hours-
Conjuring phantoms into the air
above a bar-top turned to seance table;
Of Alpine valleys echoing with cowbells,
like the ringing of distant temple gongs...
And the marketplace in Marrakesh
coming to life at Nightfall
during the month of Ramadan.

Trading stories of cheap, clean hotels
and isolated spots across 6 continents;
that have still not learned how to
prostitute their culture for the Tourists.

Information to be stored away
for when wallets lean as starving dogs
are filled again. And we can return
to all the places where we'd rather be.

RON LAMPI
THE POET'S KNOWING

In the stillness, in the silence,
in your precious moments of solitude,
so many voices come to you,
they nudge your attention,
they have so much to share with you—
You listen. You are open.
The world comes alive for you—
Yes, the world will speak in poetry,
little do others know,
but you who listens to voices
that others cannot hear, know
that the world IS poetry.
You listen. You are open.
You jot down the words & lines
you hear…

Art by KAREN KAPLAN

RON LAMPI
THESE ARE THE HORSES…

Galloping, galloping, galloping figures…
dust puffs rise up in trails across the wild open
desert plain—
They will not be captured, they will not be corralled,
they will not be tamed, they will not be put on
showcase parade for the gawking public.
Only on the wild open, eye-distant-gazing,
enormous desert plain,
the dark, agile, thrusting, noble figures
you find galloping, galloping, galloping,
free of rein, their will to roam marvelous expanses,
to roam across the primordial land,
their heads proud of origin, inviolable their build of body,
at-one-with otherworldly-like, monumental terrains,
instinctual masters of their own indominable domain—
These are the horses of the Imagination.

LADY MICHAL LAUREN
APRIL SWIRLED

We are bound to fall time, and time again,
Taking us to the great distances,
We create,
To remove ourselves from ourselves,
To seemingly play upon all the uncomfortable stages,
That we construct to be tugged at by our core.
.

Daily we cross the bridges of our unknown reaches,
We grasp for our personal star to hold our helm steady.
We nurse our desires, especially the one, just out of reach,
Waiting at the windows of our daydreams,
Under the awnings of colorful pretensions,
Wishing upon faery flowers, as we did, as children.
.

These illusions dance in and out of my radar,
In both waking and sleeping hours.
The Sirens of desire beckon.
Cafes lure me to spill ink,
While caffeinated visions amp my inhibitions.
.

I find myself often under a canopy of grief,
Weeding my personal graveyard,
Measuring all of what is buried there.
I keep finding the promise of new blooms
Even in that realm of me so long deserted.
.

There are lost treasures of me,
And, new ones to encourage to grow,
To sew these hopeful dreams into the seams
Of my new blue jeans!
No smoke screens please,
I long for what is tangible right now.
I want to remove the scrapheap
Of that which no longer serves… anything.
.

Return me, to my quest into The Mysterious.
To engage once again, childlike.
Or as a Nymph dancing in a burgeoning Rebirth.
Let me place myself into a crayon box of renewed choices.
Let me not stoop to judgement by how I appear,
Move me through the mist of the foggy misperception of beauty.
.

As much as I revel in the amber light that welcomes the night,
My sun is not ready yet to set.
I shall raise a cup of kindness to myself each dawning day,
As I continue to brew,
The ever-evolving tastes of me.

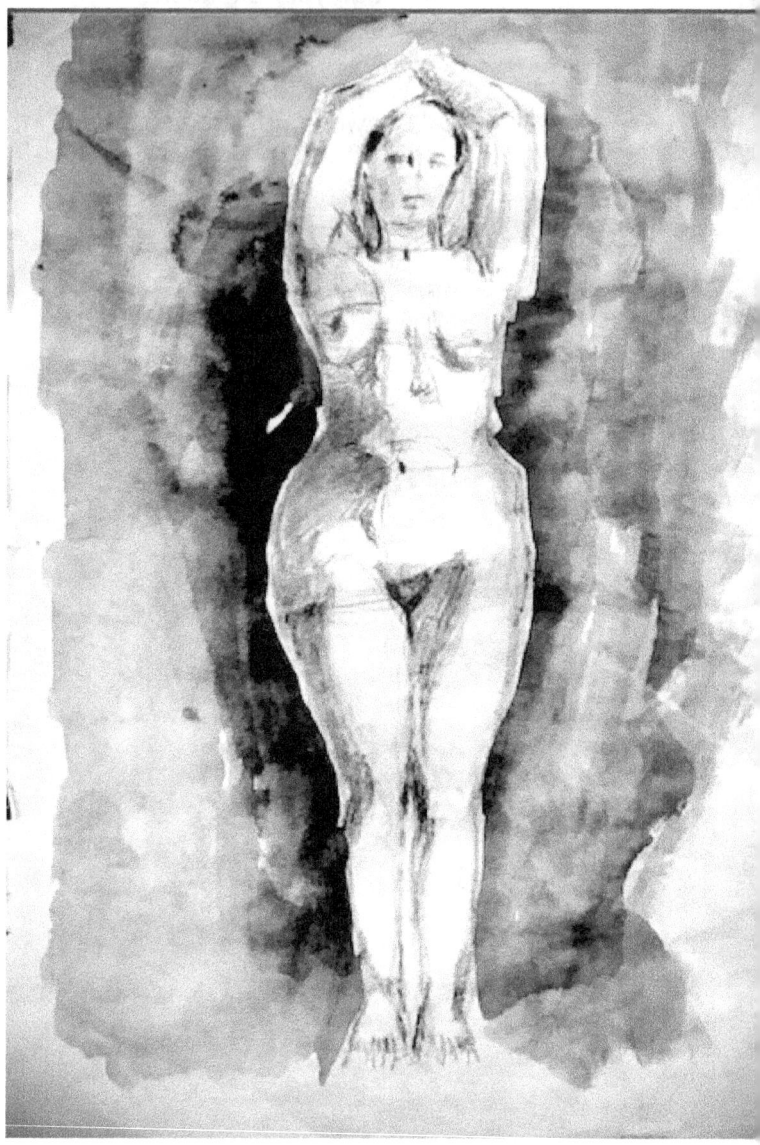

Art by LYNN ROGERS.

D.L. LANG
ROMANCING THE HOBO

If only love could pay the bills,
we'd be as rich as they come.
If only we could get by on thrills,
we'd hop the next train to freedom.

This world runs on greed and war
like we all forgot what love is for.
We must believe it will work out.
When love's involved, there is no doubt.

If only love could heal our hearts,
no two friends would ever part.
If only love became our compass,
just imagine what we'd accomplish.

Imagine what the world could be
if people were allowed to love freely.
We can see beyond our differences.
We all build upon our acts of kindness.

If only love could furnish a home,
not a soul would remain alone.
If only love could ignite our dreams,
happiness would be closer than it seems.

We spin the world a new direction
with every single act of affection.
It's just the human condition
to desire a true connection.

If only love could pay for meals,
we'd never starve for company.
If only love our hearts could heal,
the truths we would finally see.

MICHAEL LEON
THE PICTURES SHE PAINTS OF ME

long suffering the pleasure
she lusts
is a force field algorithm /
where one day is like a 1000 years /
but still can't communicate
more than a fraction of what I intend /
the picture I paint of her
takes care
of me /
her mind - her will - her heart
gives me warmth when my thoughts turn to ash /
enveloped in her subconscious presence -
unraveling
her mystery
of her
& her
placement in this world /
beyond possibility of meaning
like pagen leopards /
living & breathing
are her pictures /
painted by the sun /
not unlike the craft of a 1940s filmmaker
or a 1960s straight cop
desperate to solve his rebecka case /
innocent /
a virgin singing a lullaby/
are we not one and all
in search of the whale?

JESSICA LOOS

Bodega ate coyote and
the polka dot gum

Bang!

Blow cotton mouth
onto a drum

There's gloom in the
room like chocolate

Learn. Denver is red.

Butterflies in toast

LINDA LERNER
"A NEW YORK CORNER"
(title of a Hopper painting, 1913)

Don't believe what you see
there's the fog in the background for a reason
and the men, whose faces you can't make out
loitering around a store, whose name
you can't read… some items set out
for sale a distance from them

I see it too

the door to the store doesn't open
the men huddled by a corner they can't
get around, don't show themselves
past their black clothes, shrunk to
a floater in my eye I can't get rid of

I'm waiting for the fog to lift, to see people
enter & leave the store, sun smiling
faces reflecting my own

only that's not where I am; and
where precisely is that? I need to know,
told you, the artist doesn't say

the cost to sun this scene might have been
more than he could have afforded, no clues
to how he got to where I've also been

KIRK LUMPKIN
RE-BELL

Re-bell / re-bell / re-bell
re-member
You
are the swinging, ringing
bell of
be-ing.
Do not accept
any way of living
where you do not feel
the pulse
and tingling vibrations
from the beating heart
at the center
of the web of life
connecting all beings
in one
echoing, eco-ing,
humming, singing,
ringing
whole.
Re-bell / re-bell / re-bell
if you do not feel
down in your bones
and out to the stars,
through your every atom,
idea, and emotion
the cosmic flow
of the universal waves
of love and oneness
ringing in you,
and through you,
and from you.

"Alchemical Process" art by BOB BRANAMAN.

Re-bell / re-bell / re-bell / re-bell,
Resist, refuse, repair, re-use, recycle, restore, rejoice,
remember
You
are the swinging, ringing
bell of
be-ing.

RICK LUPERT
A DAY IN THE LIFE

Here in the
*greatest country
in the world*

kids in Wisconsin
are told not to sing
about kindness.

Meanwhile

in Nashville
a gun kills children
at another school.

This is just
one day
in America.

Photo by YARYAN

RICK LUPERT
NOT ORDINARY

A tip in a guide says *another ordinary picture
of the Eiffel Tower – Try something new.*

I wake up in Paris with that ordinary beauty
staring at me through this French window.

The way she pierces the sky and stands
assuming above everything else created

in this land of cheese and beautiful streets.
We will wander all of them today, our only

day here, like it's an infusion we've needed
for years to tide us over until the next time

we are lucky enough to *why not* our way
across the sea to this place. Monet,

we are coming for you today. Seine,
we will touch lips on your bridges.

Notre Dame, our much needed check up
after your disaster is scheduled for today.

All of it in our eyes in one day. There are no
ordinary pictures of the Eiffel Tower.

LEWIS MACADAMS
MASSIVES

Big ups to the South London soldiers
Shout-outs to Gian and Rita in Venezia,
to Michael in München,
and Harry peddling away from Der Kosmos
with Suse on his handle-bars

from LewEye at the
Truck Stops of America
in Arvin, California
as a lean citizen opines,
studying the wind-blasted hills,
"Looks like it's gonna be a helluva war,"

We're all in the beast's belly now
As it moves to establish its hegemony
across the entire planet.

                              Security?

We never asked for no
stinking security. And no,
I am not a patriot, though I'm
loyal to the Lakers,
and the L.A. River.
I am a citizen of the earth.

Poster by FITZ

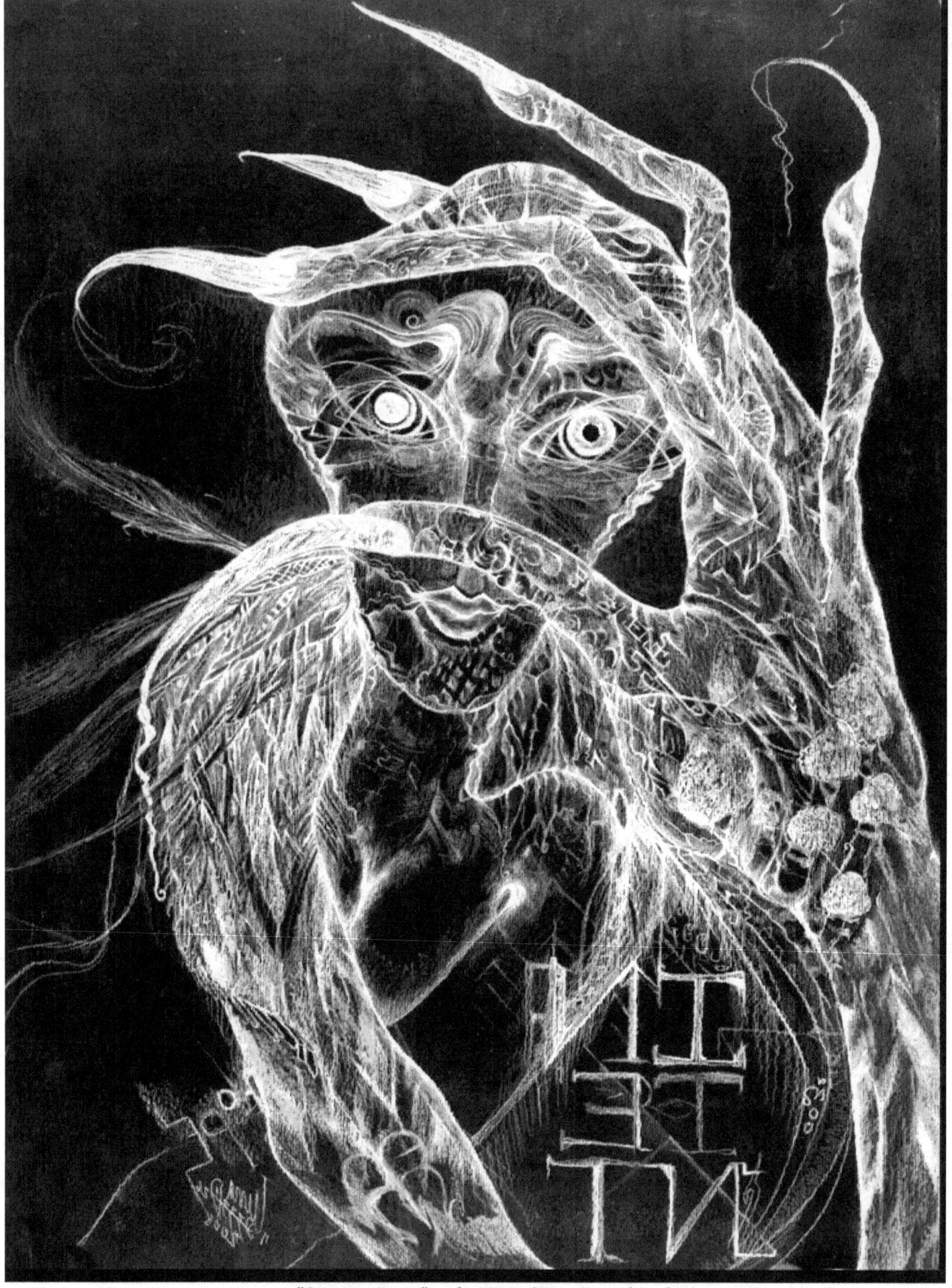

"Cognitive Intent" art by LUNA (TransSurreal Studios)

PETER MARTI
NEXUS OF A POST-BEAT LIFE

Carol was a pretty, natural blonde with a pixie cut, sparkling pale blue eyes, a lithe body and pale freckled skin. My Naropa University, Boulder, Colorado/ Kerouac School of Disembodied Poetics classmate Ron R., now Carol and her boyfriend D.'s roommate, introduced us at a dinner party I was hosting in my $75/ month basement studio apartment at 21st and Castro streets, in San Francisco, California.

It was October, 1980. That year was the perfect nexus of time, place, people, and circumstance for me—a rare moment in one's life the ancient Greeks called kairos—and was the year my life began to make sense. I was 26. When I was 13, I had discovered that alcohol cured my shyness around girls and, since then, an ever-increasing obsession with "Sex and Drugs and Rock 'n Roll" stoked delusions of grandeur. I felt like I'd somehow "earned" my sense of entitlement, yet I hadn't really done much in that regard. I was you might call an egomaniac with low self-esteem. At Naropa, back in the summer of 1977, I had studied with the well-known Beat writers like Ginsberg, Corso, and Burroughs and I wanted to be around them to absorb, in some undefined way what they had, and to shine accordingly. For example: Gregory Corso was currently my house-guest.

Vinny Z. had recommended that Gregory stay with me because, at that time, I had what I thought a nearly inexhaustible connection for the narcotic Dilaudid—how that came to pass is a whole other story…

Gregory already knew me from that past July's International Poetry Festival in Rome, when I'd scored morphine ampules for him, and also from the class he taught at Naropa in '77. Corso was the ultimate autodidact. During our six-week course on "Beowulf," he had little patience for those of us who hadn't yet read enough of the Classics he regularly referred to. He routinely dismissed his class—attended mostly by men—earlier than scheduled if he grew bored by us, or if nobody had a joint to light. I told Vinny that I thought Gregory didn't like me much.

"No, no, Lad…Gregory remembers you. He's looking forward to hanging out with you and getting high. I told him you'd pick him up at the YMCA, down on the Embarcadero, tomorrow morning. He's broke and has to move out of his room there before noon."

In the last year or so, Vinny had begun to make a rep in NYC as a purveyor of quality drugs, of some-

"Yes I did not" art by JERRY KAMSTRA

one who managed to stay high without succumbing to the more socially unattractive aspects of needle life. He was becoming the go-to dealer to the Beat and Post-Beats, and Gregory knew where his arm was buttered.

In the '40s and '50s, writers like W.S. Burroughs, Hubert Huncke and, of course, Corso had popularized glamorized and fetishized getting high—in spite of the health risks and their well-chronicled run-ins with the law. The largest population boom in the history of the world occurred after WWII, and a large percentage of that generation was now coming of age, ready to follow the Beats, Timothy Leary, Ken Kesey, The Grateful Dead, et al onto the "tune in-turn on-drop out" bus headed for everyone's mythic Free State of Cosmic Consciousness.

New York, the fiscally bankrupt City That Never Sleeps, was shattered and in decline, and an attitude of nothing's-real-everything-is-permitted permeated whatever artistic scene you could find. The LES was ground zero for scoring drugs, and Vinny lived on 2nd Avenue and St. Mark's Place. Pre-gentrification, there were dozens of abandoned buildings that coke and heroin dealers took over down there. There were boarded-up windows in those

CONTINUED NEXT PAGE

buildings that, if you knocked 'shave and a haircut' (but without the 'two bits'), an old plastic bucket was lowered by rope from an upstairs window. You put your $ in (in multiples of $10), and they raised the basket then quickly lowered it again with your order. Those little glassine envelopes the heroin was packaged in sometimes had a piece of colored tape sealing it, or they were stamped with a particular dealer's brand, like Downtown, Poison, or my favorite—Toilet. On a street like Rivington in what was known as Alphabet City, people looking to score milled about the street, asking if there were certain brands around. Other times total strangers would converge on a particular building, seemingly at random, line up and wait for a door to open and for one customer at a time to be admitted. You'd say what you wanted, the gang guys inside would ask to see your needle tracks if they didn't recognize you, and then you'd get your drugs and be taken through the blacked out, gutted building to a back courtyard where you were dismissed to a different street from where you entered.

Heroin represented the ultimate nihilistic choice for reckless scenesters, and some of us couldn't resist putting that needle in our arms, if only to experiment. Since I survived, I remember the pre-AIDS, pre-Opioid Epidemic, pre-Fentanyl-cut heroin then as mostly pure, potent and, in retrospect, still relatively "safe" for those of us who didn't want to be average, middle-class white kids.

Oh, you could die, but wasn't that part of the high?

I was a pretty decent cook and enjoyed throwing dinner parties. There was plenty of food the night I met Carol and D., but Corso was the obvious center of attention. As always, there was a gallon of good cheap California red wine to drink, and Gregory was directing the passing back-and-forth of my backyard-grown pot, two joints at a time, around and around the big oak dinner table. Carol took care to compliment me on the pasta and shyly offered to help me clean up in the kitchen during all the talk.

Afterwards, as we all headed downhill towards something—a bar or somebody's poetry reading—Gregory sidled up to me and said: "Ohhhh, Petah, your girlfriend M.—she has a great ass! You think she'd let me fuck her?"

I was surprised, not only because of Corso's directness, but because I was looking further downhill, past M., who was talking to someone, to where Carol was walking arm-and-arm with D., who was shorter than her by several inches.

"Maybe we can have a three-way; waddya think, Petah?"

I don't know man, I guess I could ask her. Gregory made a few more comments about how turned-on he was by my girlfriend. At that time, I had actually been growing more and more disenchanted with M., who had a penchant for finding my stash of drugs while I was out with my friends listening to music in clubs and bars (and looking for her replacement), and putting as much as she could up her nose. But I wasn't so sure I wanted to watch her fuck somebody else just yet.

"You're a beautiful guy, Petah Mahti," Gregory said, joshing my shoulder, "C'mon, it'll be fun." M., as it turned out, didn't want a three-way with gargoyle Gregory—news of which he took with a shrug later that night, searching for a fresh vein in his foot to shoot-up the dissolved Dilaudid tablet I had doled out. I was still stuffed, stoned, and fairly drunk from the evening, so wouldn't be joining him, but Gregory had an iron constitution. Once the syringe had filled, blossomed, and emptied into a vein in his foot, Corso became almost animated as he cleaned his works at the bathroom sink, spritzing pink blood-water on my poster, photography, and art covered bathroom wall. He seemed to take careful aim at Jack Hirschman's pro-Soviet collage/poems.

A week later, Carol and D. reciprocated by inviting me to their place for dinner. The "Naropa Issue" of my magazine Birthstone had come out and they had offered to take copies back to New Jersey City to distribute for me when they moved back there at the end of the month. Ron greeted me at the door and showed me around their sparsely furnished Mission District apartment. Carol and D. both seemed nervous or flustered, when we walked in the kitchen—like they had been just fighting maybe. Gregory was no longer my house-guest by then, having also found one of my stashes of drugs and $35 in cash that he promptly stole and vanished with.

"I only took that which you could afford to give," he wrote by way of apology. I was outraged and immediately called to complain to Vinny in NYC.

"Lad, remember: Gregory is a junkie—it's just what junkies do—he didn't mean to hurt your feelings. Look, we'll talk more when I see you there next week."

Carol kept smiling at me during dinner. I told them all about Corso "ripping me off" and I think Carol made some unkind comment about the food that D. had prepared. I could feel the tension be-

CONTINUED NEXT PAGE

Art by H. Skye Y.

CONTINUED FROM LAST PAGE

tween them, so I got Ron talking about his weird diet that involved eating only once a day—a huge meal in the evening—but nothing in-between. Then I announced that I'd be working for the radio host/music promoter Paul Rat at a Cabaret Voltaire concert at the 10th St. Catholic Church Hall in a few nights and invited them to the show, saying I'd get them on the guest list.

Paul Rat was a cool guy to work for except, of course, he didn't pay you. Since I had a good day job, I didn't really care about the $ because I loved the whole club scene, and 1980 was a magical time for music in San Francisco. Local bands like Flip-

per, the Dead Kennedys, the Looters, played often, and NYC bands like Blondie, Talking Heads, Television toured here, as did all the British bands. All I had to do was show up an hour early, set up some chairs and tables ahead of the concert, and look like I was working there.

The night of the show I was backstage, making sure nobody was sneaking in the back door, when Carol and D. showed up without Ron, who didn't like Techno Pop bands. D. soon left in a huff after Carol came and sat on my lap backstage. We were snorting out of the glass vial I always carried, and started making out. Clearly something beyond me was happing between them as a couple, but I—full

CONTINUED NEXT PAGE

of myself and oblivious to other people's feelings—just thought it was because I had good drugs and was better looking than D.—what was the big deal? After he left, Carol and I sneaked out back in the courtyard and fucked on the lawn under a statue of the Virgin Mary.

Vinny Z. had left rainy NYC to spend a few weeks in sunny California, and was at my place when I arrived home later. I told him about my night, about Carol and D. and M., and how complicated my feelings were. He was his usual, non-judgmental self. Later, like 40 years later, he said to me: "I've never met anyone who could justify, literally, anything they do, quite like you," words that would've had zero ef-

---

"I called Vinny 'The Doctor' because I never could stomach actually shooting drugs into my own veins..."

---

fect on me in 1980.

Vinny was also in SF to visit the writer Simone Lazzeri Ellis, whom he'd met at Naropa, and who by then was attending the Art Institute studying film. Vinny and I, like everyone in Boulder in 1977, was in love with the beautiful Simone, whom I'm sure didn't know we existed then. By 1980 though Vinny had, through his ability to find the right drugs for the right people, and Gregory's connections, gained access to the upper echelons of various NYC artistic cliques. Bedding Simone was quite a feather for Vinny. A few days later, sitting in my kitchen, she read to us her beautifully written story about a street-whore she'd befriended who, dressed in hot-pants, crop-top, and platform shoes, walked the Grand Canyon all the way down and back up in one day, which took something like 15 hours of continuous hiking. Simone's writing was full of detail and pathos and humor and it became part of her book "In the Vernacular."

D. left their apartment early to drive their stuff back to Jersey in their big Ford station wagon. Carol and I managed to spend most of the next night together there, after which Ron gave me a hard time about it, taking D.'s side, declaring it my fault they broke up. He was bemoaning the loss of two paying roommates—even though they were both leaving anyway—and that he had to find another place to live.

Somehow M., in spite of my denials, figured out what had happened (probably through Ron) and, while I was at work, infiltrated the enemy's camp. The two of them, both unemployed at the time, met up and got day-drunk and decided to apply for stripper jobs at The Garden of Eden—one of the North Beach clubs.

By the next week though, I was dropping Carol at the airport in my work van. She was moving to NYC to join the Exploding Garbage Can Band or to get into an artist's loft or something. Smitten, I asked if I could visit her once she settled in and she promised to call me.

Carol's New York, LES studio was on Ave. C off Rivington Street, and had a bathtub in the middle of the slopping kitchen floor, where we soaked with Heinekens and talked about the sex afterwards. A weak, late Spring sun crept across the wall trying to find us. To my worry that I hadn't made her come, she quoted Henry Miller: "I like what he says—that there's too much emphasis on the clit."

That trip pops up vivid all these years later for a couple of pictures I found recently, using M.'s nice Nikon, that I snapped of Carol in Vinny's Second Ave. flat. She had on a brown suede jacket and shyly looked down at her hands in one photo, and then brightly up in another, smiling at something someone said. Later that night, Vinny shot us both up with Downtown—a retail brand of heroin popular in Alphabet City that week. As far as I know, that was the first time she'd had heroin. I called Vinny "The Doctor" because I never could stomach actually shooting drugs into my own veins, which I credit with saving me from the fate of several friends and acquaintances over the next few years, though I did end up with Hep C that went undiagnosed for 20 years.

I returned to SF to live with M. in a much bigger flat upstairs from my basement studio. Carol's phone got disconnected and a letter I wrote was returned. After another year of near-constant fighting, M. moved out and back to her parents in Brooklyn. Twenty years later, Carol's ex-boyfriend D. was still publishing his own, much longer-lived poetry magazine than Birthstone ever was. He also wrote a bitter, tell-all memoir/ novella, about his and Carol's relationship, and about that time in the fall of 1980 when our lives intersected and I thought everything was great. He said it was my fault they broke up, and also blamed me because Carol had gone on to mainlining the LES heroin on her own, got an embolism from it, and died a year or so after that

CONTINUED NEXT PAGE

bath we took—which was the last time I saw her.

D.'s memoir captured Carol's personality, intelligence, and beauty—along with his anger at me—which was difficult to read about. For a long time, I had forgotten just how I first heard about Carol's death. See, D. actually did write me shortly after she died in the hospital, which he described in great detail. At the time, I was able to take that in and pretend that nothing was wrong that everything was cool, that Carol was a casualty of war, just another fallen fellow soldier, whom I'd known a little bit…

Partly this was due to my current circumstances. I was newly in love and living with another natural blonde, L., who was a classically trained pianist. I was busy working day jobs as a roofer, painter, demo guy, and cook. Nights I was with L., writing practicing playing music. I stopped selling drugs and even doing them much. But I also couldn't acknowledge the truth of my own addictions and the consequences of my behavior.

"The Denial is strong in this one," Lord Vader breathes.

L.'s job at the time was bartender at the Hotel Utah, the historic South of Market watering hole a few blocks from the 6th and Bryant Police Headquarters. Framed and autographed pictures of Joe DiMaggio, Marilyn Monroe, and other icons on the wall. A sweet Vietnamese couple served inexpensive bar-food. It was our watering hole/ hiring hall/ venue. Our band, Arms of Venus played there a few Fridays or Saturdays a month. Dennis, the young tall good-looking manager there, introduced us to P., an Italian stewardess who became our roommate. One night, shortly after she moved in, she had a party at our new flat on 18th and Noe that started after L. and I had already gone to bed for the night. P., her boyfriend, and Dennis and his girlfriend Sue Mutant, had apparently all done heroin and were up and down for hours, laughing, talking and throwing up in the bathroom next to where we were trying to sleep. In the morning P. was appropriately apologetic for all the noise, saying: "Yeah, I tried

"Hare Core" art by LUNA (TransSurreal Studios)

that stuff but I don't want to be paying money just to throw up a perfectly good meal."

I usually threw up on heroin too, and never sought out the drug in SF, preferring to let it be an NYC thrill. Besides, L. was adamant about me being gainfully employed and fully functional. She had had a boyfriend for a while (a semi-famous guitarist in a local band) who never paid his share, always being drug-broke.

A few months after that late-night vomit-fest, her boss Dennis OD'd and his body was shipped back to somewhere or Kansas. There was no SF memorial except for our raised boilermakers, sitting at the Utah bar.

It was around that time I got D.'s letter blaming me for Carol's death, which I threw out. I didn't want L. to know about that particular bit of my history. It didn't make me look cool.

ELLYN MAYBE
SOMEDAY OUR PEACE WILL COME

one day poetry dropped from the sky
and the animals grew iambic pentameter tails
and the people breathed in stars

one day music dropped from the sky
and the architecture turned symphonic
and the people breathed in harmony

one day memory dropped from the sky
and the past present and future sifted like flour
and the people breathed in wonder

smoke and ash
as distant as two sides of the same coin

Originally written and published for S.A. Griffin's project,
The Poetry Bomb

KRIS MILLER

Press the start button on the door you
came into this existence. Reset the
game to times of total immersion in the
moment. Mere mortals cannot compete
for attention, when games bombard the
senses of sight, sound, shaking,
motions, risk, elation. The aroma of hot
lights, electric solenoids, overheated
electric circuitry. Ding Ding, indicates
which floor of the Twilight Zone you are
on.

RICHARD MODIANO
ON THE LOWER EAST SIDE

I didn't land in NYC's Lower East Side
until I was in my 20s

Then home to La Mama, the Nuyorican Poets Cafe,
the Grassroots Tavern, the SWP headquarters,
339 Lafayette Street where CORE, the War Resisters League,
the Socialist Party and the Free Association
were housed under one roof
and the NYC General Membership Branch
of the IWW at 119 E. 10th Street a couple of doors
from St. Mark's in the Bowery and the Poetry Project

Though told that the LES was in an
advanced state of disintegration
it was so much livelier than anything I
had known before that I found it
hard to imagine how it could have
been better even though the
neighborhood was hard hit by crime

I had the unparalleled experience
of fraternity, life on the LES was
the closest thing to living anarchism
it has ever been my pleasure
to enjoy despite battles with landlords,
harassment by cops and muggers

The artists who lived there and their allies,
old time Bowery bums, sex workers, drug-addicts,
winos, gays and lesbians
and other outcasts, maintained a vital
community based on mutual aid and in which
being different was an asset rather than a liability

In this society, made of many races and ethnicities,
the practice of solidarity and equality was second
nature -- almost everyone was poor,
but no one went hungry, and newcomers
had no trouble finding a place to stay

On the Lower East Side of the 1970s
what mattered most was poetry,
freedom, creativity, and having a good time

To paraphrase an old aristocrat, "Those who
did not live before the gentrification
will never know how sweet
life was"

3/27/22

MIKE M. MOLLETT

DANCING OUR LIVES AWAY

for all the poets & friends forever before us / forever after (re-worked 7/23)

Who is at the doors of knockabout history

with fiery language burning translations?

it's us and our visionary ancestors   friends, mentors,

fallen angel gurus   shooting

a new kind of apple with new music tweets & shit

into our systems' dialogue - the mind's alley eye corner with

heads energizing in some wild cooking groove... LISTEN...

the airs are full of info-bites, short-cut texting,

new genres of canned cool memes & singing gifs popping-up

what a world! posting oozy sandwich-like confetti conversations.

shit, we all do it ok? this way & that more & less like...

what an adventure in quilting!   within

the itching open stage of ISness   where we live in

this swirling bit of the creation myth   each time.

there's cacophony with the crowd chorus of us (& this is cool)

sort of symphonic resonant & noise rambling

          we may like this   like this a lot

Thank you happy face!

Yea, tho I walk thru the Valley of...Life.

          Performance Art Today!

Maybe we can figure this out together....

   as we're all in some transition...

grab a six-pac of whatever suits you LOL

There's no intermission in this dance.

sniff & sip the scrumptious scene

the landforms too will read all about it

uploading contemporary jpegs of soul with

tooth-cracking outbursts of rage from the windows' fingertips...

there's a long history here in the making...

I am actually not just a little crazy in this flow

with each breaking news bundle meme...

you name it   you fill it in

more trouble for the juicy mind

It can be so delicious...   CONTINUED NEXT PAGE

in this pop-up mosh-pit as I reach
beyond fucking 70
on this planet thing called EARTH
state of being

Who's next for the trophy?

step right up!
we've got Mr. Megalomania - the hairdoo once head of state
a madman cornucopia of delusion born to sneer...
flash-tweeting messages of hate   yes siree...
dignitaries & common me's are included in his rants.
it's not at all that hilarious anymore   this joy-sucking
gut-like wall of stupid must-be petro nonsense.
it doesn't get any better on this planet
for the rotten side of the ill-picked fruit

Shut the fuck up!
billions of us species are at risk in this grey-lit sky   no lie
this is the sad bag truth   you know...
believe me   trust me   like me
no masks of encryption can protect any of us anymore
in the rubble of thinking
near the flames & floods of apocalypse
we teeter & totter with fractured faces assuming balance
What a pallid empty bubble
clouds circling & squaring from mouths' made-up mantras...
all of us are in the sway   OR ELSE...

STOP!   TAKE THIS QUIZ NOW:
                  How do you spell E N V I R O N M E N T ?
when L O V E seems to be loosing all nourishing value?

take a right   a right   a right right right
take a cellphone breather   take a nap
3 dancing our lives away   mm

shop amazon   google   wall street   porn
sell the Real Truth   buy crypto   we've got

CONTINUED NEXT PAGE

"War of Wealth" art by T. MIKE WALKER.

MOLLETT CONTINUED FROM LAST PAGE

the drugs sex booze guns

we've got the lobbyists

we've got the senators

we've got the lies   the demagogues   the holy.

who needs a ticket   red state   blue state

      when we have the Couch of Pervasive Oblivion ...

Oh, Man, Woman, step away jump!

This thing-LIFE is a holy celebration.

listen up without worry I muse to myself

& to those with edible ears…like you with eyes clear & winking

read the lips bleeding green & softly

touch your neighbor in sensitive spots in the wondrous

osmotic tintinnabulation of heart   WE DO SHARE

      there where we can dream easy wild & bright

          & drown

            & dance

              & SING

        in this crazy incomprehensible...

Yes sing & dance   chant & stretch

      vibrate & rave our lives

           away

K.R. MORRISON
ELECTIONS

i pick poets

i pick girls who slay
guitars, i pick women
who spit in his ego face

i pick kids
who can pick your pocket
who also carry
a single mother's groceries

i want the mother tired
of being tired, while her children
visit father graves, engraving
new, revolutionary sons

i pick the fighter, the vagrant
the sick, the manic
Joan of Arc
i pick her treason
her holy mistakes

i pick the wounded
who elections later, the masses praise
when history suits them

i pick my brother's backyard
i choose my sister's shotgun seat
a baretta on the floorboard, by her feet

i pick men who insist on revising
their masculine, i pick families
who revere what's feminine
i pick men who mother
soothe & nourish their nests

i pick bare, calloused feet
that walk away from this suicide
we call the United States

        i choose to awaken to new
        love, to healed generations

            i pick love pure, i pick poetry
                whispering from outlaw sidewalks

K.R. MORRISON
SUBMIT

There's a dead version of me
who craves you

        your calloused hand
                choking
                        my neck

        spit in my mouth

        you demand
        the burn of a bite arousing
        me wet, tears & teeth tearing
        my moonflesh

That wounded girl is gone.

I burned her alive
at sea, sent her
into Hekate shadows
hungry for a hawkmoth, rising

        Kiss me
        with your strongest parts
        without fractured bones
        of your own boy wounds

        Peel off these ghosts, hold me
        where my secrets show
        scarlet fire graffiti branded
        in lady caves deep inside
        of me, I am
                a mess
                        of avalanches

        Breathe your oak
        tree arms into me
        if you want
        to bite, taste all of me
                swallow
                        my scars

My landmines are gone.
Don't ask for my consent to hurt me.

HARRY E. NORTHUP
NEEDED RAIN

I should never of others, but my own

O, Lord, I am frail & fallen
& fear I should appear strong & confident
& I break down & cry a dozen times a day

I have no one to be with me in poetry,
Each step, except when I wrote -- my wife

O, Lord, help me accept my imperfections
Distance me from my escapes
Make my face a mask of greenery

It's too rainy to go to the chapel
This song is my bewilderment
I deny what I love
Words lead me in waking
I am part of loss & love
Behind the magnolia tree by the chapel

Where do I go, O, Lord?
To stay warm & dry & hopeful, I pray
Love scolds me & never stops

11 8 22

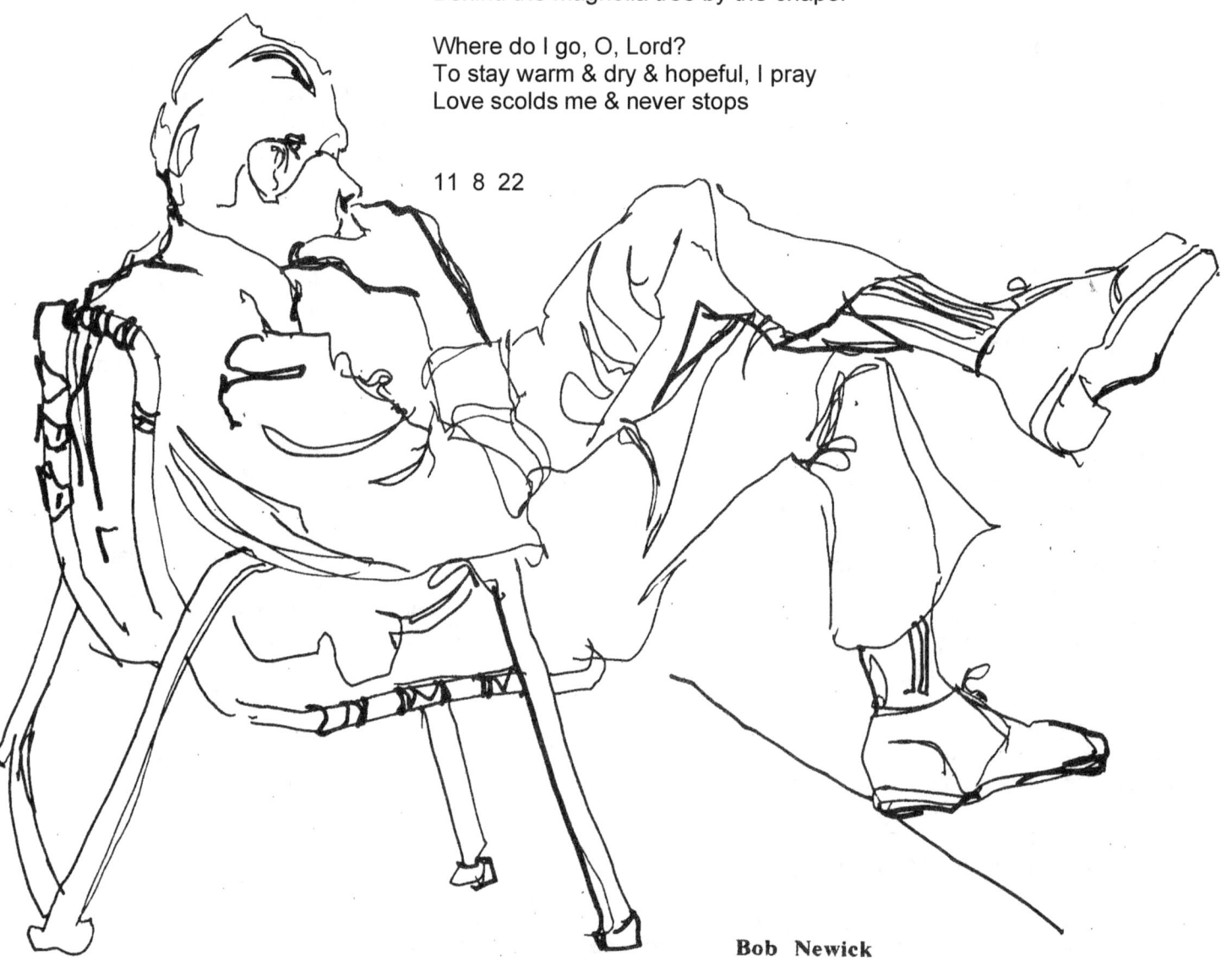

Bob Newick

PHILLIP T. NAILS
LETTER TO A WEBSITE

Phillip T. Nails performing at Sparring With Beatnik Ghosts in the basement of Li Po Lounge, San Francisco on August 23, 2008. Photo by YARYAN.

Dear Ecstasy,
I see on the information highway
a super storm of bliss
wetting my eyes and making my hungry bones smile.

I perceive a spirit levitating
like fire suspended in mid moan.
In my memory there is a caress
that brings technicolor understanding.
My hand on your heart, your heart against my palm,
your fingers, defining the arteries of my soul
at the center of my chest pumping desire
like vintage motor.
Your curvature inspires the burning sun.
A heat emanates from your lips.
I can see it in your photographs,
feel its presence in the universe.

I too have rolled in the sand
wanting to soak up the earth
with my fragility, my patient want.
You are a favorite song and
repetition is key strokes on burgundy typewriter
spelling wishes that sync to jazz.
Horns blowing, speaking sadness only you can solve,
a balm on my crude mind
you whisper electric poems across my manual undertaking.
Please, may I be in your world if just for a little while,
may I pet the air you walk in.
I'd love to be next to you like a cat staring
into your eyes, every invitation holding still while
the planets turn and stars reflect you. That is the light, that is the big bang,
shining when you glance in my direction.
Do you wanna pull my hair?

SPARRING WITH BEATNIK GHOSTS
OMNIBUS

Editor: **DANIEL YARYAN**   *Mystic Boxing Commission*   *Vol.1, Jan. 2022*   Michael C Ford Edition

BRENNAN
BUKOWSKI
CHEN
COLEMAN
COOK
DE LA VEGA
EVERSON
FERLINGHETTI
HAND
HARRIS
HIGGENBOTTOM
HIRSCHMAN
KAMSTRA
LAMBERT
MAMACOATL
MARCUS
MCADAMS
MCGOWAN
MELTZER
MICHELINE
MOE
PRADO
RIOS
RUSSO
SALAS
STOLPE
STORTI
TEXIDOR
VINOGRAD
WANNBERG
WEISS
WEISSER

Plus More...

Featured Cover Artist: T. Mike Walker   *Book Designer: Yaryan*

**SPECIAL FEATURE
FROM RON LAMPI:**   *Daniel's Vision*   A Poem Chronicle of
Sparring With Beatnik Ghosts

SPARRING WITH BEATNIK GHOSTS OMNIBUS is available at Lulu.com and www.sparringartists.com

Gerald Nicosia at Sparring in Mill Vallley, CA at Sweetwater Music Hall, 2013. Photo: YARYAN

GERALD NICOSIA
REVIEW: SPARRING WITH BEATNIK GHOSTS OMNIBUS

I have been reading poetry anthologies and collections for fifty years, but I've never seen anything quite like the SPARRING WITH BEATNIK GHOSTS OMNIBUS. The Beat Movement transformed American literature and American life, but, strangely, no one has ever really put a fence around it and showed it fully, in all its true colors. Daniel Yaryan's OMNIBUS finally does this for us. Don Allen's NEW AMERICAN POETRY did this in a small way at the start of the Beat Movement, but then things went wild, and Beat started to transform all of American life with the hippie movement, sexual liberation, Pop Art, and in a thousand other ways. To show where Beat has gone in art one needs more than just poetry, one needs paintings, photos, activist rants, and poetry of every radical description. It's all here in the OMNIBUS, the old Beat pioneers like Ferlinghetti, McClure, Kamstra, Meltzer, and Micheline, the Beat stalking horses like Bukowski, weiss, and Everson, and the younger generation of writers whose minds and literary styles had been permanently blown by the Beat revolution as if it were the original acid—writers like Wannberg, Doug Knott, Clausen, Wanda Coleman, Pamela Twining, Stephen Kessler, and even myself, who was permanently expelled from the academic world when I ran smack into Beat. There will never be another collection like the OMNIBUS. This giant beautiful book has the goods. It gives the full spectrum of Beat in all its shimmering psychotropic magnificence. It will change the life of anyone who reads it, like Beat has changed all of us forever.

> --Gerald Nicosia, author of MEMORY BABE: A CRITICAL BIOGRAPHY OF JACK KEROUAC, HOME TO WAR, and BEAT SCRAPBOOK

Marc Olmsted at Sparring in Berkeley, CA, 2010. Photo: YARYAN

MARC OLMSTED
WISDOM CRIMINALS ON THE LAM

a rosary punched out of a skull
dark flaming wrathful deities on my wall
- must be Satanist pin-up centerfolds of depravity!
"Ms. May likes flayed human skin & long walks in the sky"
- arrest me! I confess
I'm a dada phantom vigilante
a nude Buddha protector policing the greed
defund my concepts
cancel anger
eat the heart of my own importance
shackle me in light!
can I have a cell facing East?
I'll dream of Tibet
mind hero in my own non-existent movie
autocrat rulers of thuggish reactions
I now sentence to calm & liberation
my id got lost
I can't afford the new I-phone
Give me 3 hots & a cot and
a nice big
blank wall   5/3/22

MARC OLMSTED
CRUSH

How I embarrassed myself
when young with
mad crushes &
ridiculous schemes
revealed poems
notes of desperate honesty –
once even tried to
retrieve a letter from
the street corner mailbox
sticking
in my hand
(no luck) –

now how
many are
dead?

3/1/21

SUZI KAPLAN OLMSTED
TOUCHDOWN JESUS IS GONE

It used to be visible for miles,
arms raised toward the heavens,
announcing victory.

Around the Ohio church,
this statue was a landmark.
Area residents enjoyed seeing it
day after day.

"Touchdown" Jesus, they called it.
Highway 75 had little else of note and
it was always good to be reminded of one's faith.

Lightening struck Jesus' right hand, and he caught fire.

Area resident Cassie Browning tried to reassure,
"The statue of Jesus can be destroyed, but Jesus can't,"
though another resident
who used to stop at the statue
at least once a week
told onlookers,
"I just don't understand what God is up to.
It just doesn't make
any sense."

Suzi Kaplan Olmsted June 2010

"Jesus on a Bicycle" art by TRACY WITT

SUZI KAPLAN OLMSTED
HEAT DOME

Watching the news with the captions on
29 million under heat alert
The blonde news lady tells us
We're going to have "temperatures 10-15 degrees higher for this time of year"
(But the captions say "tomb of year," Marc points out)
Heat dome over us
I'm in my sweltering near term extinction broken air conditioner heat dome house
If not my tomb, my likely place to die
I'm not enjoying the early part of the apocalypse
Undone by a week of deprivation of one luxury
My badassery restricted to my "Naked & Afraid" fandom: A knife, a pot, a Fire starter
While I eat a bag of chips, drinking an icy cold Coca Cola
In a glass bottle
Because, you know, it's better for the environment

JANE ORMEROD
CHICKEN HEART

Tankage for dry lot? Lightweight pigs make less rapid gains? Fancy singing to sirens or the homicide squad?

This is late. It is big. It is Doric column. Party trick or floating body. It is birthday, it is grind. Palm tree on fire. Settle or sell or twist? Oh yeah, it's the cutest thing. A re-hash, a trite mix of Joyce and Dostoevsky. Chicken heart.

Capture failing laughs in the best port barrel. Tell me, are you honest? A honey? A dying chimp waiting for gravy? Hawk, post, open, smirk, go to waste or be crazy. Be crazy as a house, become my littlest pony.

Choose homicide.

The pennies on my eyes came from nowhere. The music inside myself goes unnoticed. I cannot move without galoshes. I cannot compare myself to camel hair, to an unlocked door, padding, tiling, that bakery I used to own. The girl over there is wrong, the pony is an accordion, and the myself is the music of a paper boat as beautiful as the arm of the tenth stranger.

Again, that old sobbing, the drink call in the morning, the stink call of the word *go*, the stray conjunction of happiness and happiness is evening happiness is bridge and wax and fish and the happiness of a darling, darling, darling, darling, darling, darling. The articles of breakfast and lunch, the prescriptions and turkey, the cardinal principle of philanthropy, and the itch for a new name and hotter-than-ever cakes.

Yes, rain is foolish gold, a foolish plot for any reader. Drowsing the alleys, the face is the heel of the body. Is a saying of never having to worry over the growing light inside the refrigerator you bought your mother when your first record went gold.

INDIANA PEHLIVANOVA
GHOST GROKKING

Art by H. Skye Y.

I wonder about ghost's dreams
Do they dream in pink or grayscale?

Do they get nosebleeds,
get bruised?

Do they get upset
leaving smudged fingerprints everywhere?

I wonder if ghosts remember
how to spell
How to ride a bicycle
How to read a map

Do all people who die in fires
go to the same place?
I imagine a deep watering hole
to cool off their third-degree burns

Are ghosts stuck in their own micro-universes
of cacophonous grief?

Are ghosts neatly arranged by eye color
arrayed in a larger universe
like bubbles rising
in a glass of water?

JOSE ANTONIO PINEDA
SHAMAN
(DEDICATED TO MICHAEL MCCLURE)

He stands on the cliff above the promontory the hills above the sea, wolves stand watch mushrooms
and funghi grow in the cemetery as cats copulate under trees, birds eggs hatch

His head is wreathed in fiery thunderbolts Shaman, progeny of rainclouds and sun one day your soul
will pass on to stars that diamond the onyx night time skies

Drink of loves philtre of divine fungi emerge shining one from subterranean cave onto winged chariot
of the sun and fly above lands Mediterranean

You escaped prisons of bars and barbed wire free to wander the road to heaven or hell you roam
city streets searching for love you await the holy one, bringer of dawn

Serpentine hair adorns her leonine profile as she harvests fungi and mushrooms to trespass
treasure troves of dreams and sail past the pyramids by the Nile

Shaman, your road is blue and near done half devil half angel you followed the sun down times
dusty highway traveled far to worship the dawn of the morning star

Artwork by DANIEL O. STOLPE -- from the Kamstra Sparchive Collection.

KUSHAL PODDAR
NOIR TEMPLE

From the firmament, imagine,
the steeple looks like a ship
ready to leave the planet decaying.

You joke, "It is the tip of your confession."
My sins laugh aloud. We have buried
silence beneath the bits of the bottles
thrown away. No one steps downhill.
People, even the temple, use it as a bin.

One night the edifice disappears.
The fright tightens its grip.
Is the end nearing? Now that the land
lies vacant will the words hushed
and flesh rotten surface?

KUSHAL PODDAR
MAZE

The day I name the way
a maze
it begins to own a bit of me,
and I lay
my claim on a patch of its length
that circles
an overgrown shrub, the time-eaten wall
and a shameless body of muddy water.

At one point
I feel the desire to leave the maze
drying, dying.
From hollow in my abdomen
an eclipse of moths swirl out.

The sun relents;
crickets croon some troubled Sinéad.
On a rock I sit.
Again I walk, stumble upon a upturned
perambulator.
Shadows ebb and tide once more.
I recall the time
my body used to grow and the point
it stopped.

JOHN PUSEY
BROTHERS IN ARMS

I've been on this road for ages now
Marching with my brothers in arms
Our weapons are hammered from dreams and visions
Not broadsword steel or hipshot lead
Our songs celebrate our great defeats
And the last shreds of hope are the tattered banners
We hold high

There is nothing trivial about our losses
The universes we've been forced to abandon
Giving ground only at the bitter end
Voting with the one good eye or fingertip
In favor of retreat
A concession to buy more time
As we regroup

Huddled here, under a bright but empty sky
I see more shadows than solid forms
Our ranks have been diminished
As the threads of time unwind
And our ropes and tackle, worn thin and rusted
As we haul ourselves up one more Palisade
Begin to fail

As the Jester and the Fool
I sing of our lost loves
Phantom limbs and perished thoughts
Conjuring them once more
With a toast of old wine and fresh blood
In the flimsy light and curling smoke
Of a damp hemp fire

Each of us must choose our last campaign
The rest of us will come with what remains
One hand held high in grand salute
One hand held low, weighed down by love
We wear a steady gaze to behold eternity
Our thoughts embrace infinity
And our hearts surrender

Artwork by LYNN ROGERS.

KENNON B. RAINES
MY BODY, MY CHOICE

Too many people on planet Earth
We won't survive compulsive birth
Too many people non-stop consume
Driving Climate Crisis & our doom
My Body, My Choice, My Right...My Body, My Choice, My Life
My Body, My Choice, My Right...I said it's MY BODY, My Choice, My Life!
Right-to-Lifers insist on the right
Of every embryo to have life
But once that little baby arrives
Won't spend a dime to help it thrive
My Body, My Choice, My Right...My Body, My Choice, My Life
My Body, My Choice, My Right...I said it's MY BODY, My Choice, My Life!
Whether rape, incest, or poverty
"Have the baby," says the GOP.
Don't bring a child into misery
To grow up dysfunctionally
My Body, My Choice, My Right...My Body, My Choice, My Life
My Body, My Choice, My Right...I said it's MY BODY, My Choice, My Life!
Who do they think they are to say?
Whose life is it anyway?
Are we living in the land of the free?
If we are it's up to you and me!
My Body, My Choice, My Right...My Body, My Choice, My Life
My Body, My Choice, My Right...I said it's MY BODY, My Choice, My Life!

October 2022

FRANK T. RIOS
March 22, 1936 –Aug. 20, 2018

Sparring Legacies
FOOTSTEPS
OF THE WIND

FRANK T. RIOS
UNTITLED

The long night is even
longer when the vision
is hidden
& the man in black
lights the jagged scar
under the lamppost
where he loves to hang…

We gathered in a circle
canting poems
that did not rhyme
long into the long night
the music of Bird & Monk
passing the Joint
along the jagged scar

the poems wailed
Patchen & Perkoff
Corso & Rios
like a warm coat
surrounded by dying
sticking out like stumps
in a graveyard

O Lady
kiss our black pens
into the long night
where all Poets go.

A. RAZOR
IN THE DUST OF TIME WE FIND OURSELVES AS
SCATTERED PARTICLES AMONGST THE RUINS

the ratchet of joints working on bones
becoming such a clear sound against
the lonely morning backdrop of rocks
& bushes spread out atop the hot sand
as the things you think you can
remember
are lost in the shortened breaths of
a movement's cadence that calls out
for more love as if it was the last handful
of precious water brought up to the lips
as they quiver with thirst all the while
hoping to be relieved of their parched
predicament only to be moments away
from the disappointment felt as one realizes
it's too damn late to wait for, to go
somewhere else to quench that
lust for the blessing of the aquifer
for the full-bodied arrangement that
comes from living in proximity to a
source that would be helpful in order
to share the wealth of liquid freshness
that we once took for granted
like it would always be there
& now we know
                        the spring that provides
for our cultivation of an answer
in the form of a hard rain that
has no choice but to fall on us
even tho we stretch out palms
& extend our hands upwards
towards an unknown source
of the liquid life-giving wonder
that
        we
                have
                        needed
                                more & more
every day &
every night
we have spent
thirsty with an
unstabilized predilection
that all we will ever need
will be there, running down
every mountainside towards an
epic reckoning of an ebb & flow
somewhere out there in the night
where the drought might not be
over, but
                you need to have
                        hydration
before
you can understand
dying of thirst
                        completely

Photo by DANIEL YARYAN

LYNN ROGERS
HOMELESS JONES

Vibrant but grandiose dreams
Led her to deliver sermons
In downtown San Jose streets
To sleep amid pigeons outside Five Wounds
Church; it was her calling
Me late at night; "Thanks
'Rev. Rogers' for all you do,"

Which isn't much
Taking bags of discarded clothing
Outside her latest mental health Helter
Shelter; she comes along, late,
In garish painted hair, hooker style
Eyelashes askew and I ask myself
Is it worth it to give the best duds
I have when she will invariably

Lose them in a sweat-drenched whirlwind
Of rocky opportunities
Sweeping plans—
She is an evangelist
A wanderer, a true Franciscan
Who lets possessions fly

More courageous, even, than I.

LYNN ROGERS
TRUCK STOP

Jemmima snubbed her cigarette in the gravel truck yard. She looked up past the huge Jones Crossing sign, looked northeast, up Idaho way.

"You'll never leave him like this, baby," a voice spoke in her head. Mama Duvall, dead five years, still spoke to her, come morning or night—any time Jemmy needed her.

First cigarette out, no coffee yet, Jemmy shook her tanned arms and hands free from her sleep rumpled white blouse. Wore that blouse too many times as a teacher in California. No more half gassed, dropout kids for this summer, no more married, lying Matthew Haines, she was off.

Shallow sun came pale and white from behind the Jones Crossing sign. Facing east where he was, I love you I love you, came the familiar chant in her head. Give him up, she told herself, too many mornings, an empty dream.

When she saw the sun coming stronger orange down now, she crossed the long Jones Crossing yard to the diner laid along, beneath the sign.

Love you love you Matthew Haines, the words that had held her every day for two and a half years. The words ground down low into the gravel yard. She passed between long grey truck cabs and detached truck bodies. In love love, Matthew Haines, wasn't here.

He was in the goddamn Bahamas with his no sex wife Bambina.

Bambina with her dangly gold bracelets, emperor head brooch, acrid perfume. Bambina wanted more damn rocks, more damn stones, Jemmy here in front of this truck stop in her jeans and slept-in blouse had wanted to "fuck Matthew's nuts off" (he said) all night long most every night, love on him twenty-four seven, but no, he wouldn't let her.

Jemmy kicked back the truck stop screen, opened the inner door with her boot-clad foot. She came in past the rounder of tourist gizmos and took a seat. A big Indian head painting reminded her when she'd been here last. Jemmy was a crack shot, had learned that from her Uncle Gabe up Idaho way. She could blast a hole in that wooden head if she wanted.

Big clock above the Indian said 6:15 P.M. She'd been sleeping all day. Night to drive, or stay here in this dive? She took a seat at the counter. She said, "Coffee," when the burly man, asked.

The guy came back with the brew. "How long you gonna be here, Missy?"

"Ms.—Ms. Jemmina Cruso," she corrected. Then, "I dunno." Already shedding the California lingo. A night driving up through the desert did that.

"Long enough, I guess." She turned at a noise behind her.

A man in a plaid hunting jacket came through the door, sat down beside her. She stared at him. Green eyes. Wan, like an all-night drive.

"Juan McGraff, Ms. Jemmima," the big waiter announced the visitor to her. "This here's Juan McGraff. Comes but once in a while."

"So?" Jemmy hunched back over her cup. The man pushed odd bits of old silver around on the counter and looked her up and down. She could feel his eyes all over, like a brush plant blown out of darkness; he was reaching for her already.

"I didn't mean to intrude," he said.

"What'll you have?" the waiter addressed them together.

"The lady'll have corn beef and hash, scrambled eggs, whipped and cooked flat, big glass of O.J., I'll have the same," he said, "but for me add pancakes, silver syrup and butter."

"What?" She startled. He freaked her too much to get up. It was everything she wanted.

CONTINUED NEXT PAGE

"And she'll have some artificial sweet in the coffee too—weird—has it for a lift when she don't want sugar."

The hair stood out on her neck. How'd he know?

By the time the burly guy brought the stuff, she hadn't looked up at all, but only felt this guy beside her. He hadn't said anything more. The food helped.

"All right little lady, you tell me, why are you here?"

"You know it all. Tell me."

"Running from something."

She spilled, about Matthew Haines—M.H. to underlings at the Company Grand-about Bambina, the jewels, about her own struggle teaching E.S.L. to Voc. kids—her being a writer, really—a writer—a writer about all of it.

By 7:30 he had her dancing in front of the juke box.

Hands gentle behind her back, he pushed her forward and back, slow, like rocking. She wanted to fall asleep. He kept it up like that awhile through Sweet Dreams of You. He tugged her close and back some more, when You got to know when to hold 'em, know when to fold 'em, came on.

She felt her Uncle Gabe in him and the remembrance of Gabe's sun porch up northeast Idaho from here. With her own folks dead and Aunt Sandy too, she'd stayed with Gabe and Mama Duvall, in high school, before coming down to NorCal Teaching College.

Here on the no-tell dance floor with Juan, Matthew Haines was just a frigging memory. For the first time she looked at Juan. She saw up into pale eyes, green like a Wichita street, green like a sweep of California sea lichen at low tide, green like the spring leaves of a Salmon River forest.

Around Juan's green-lit gaze she caught the rest, the weather-worn features, strong chin and jaw, lean tanned neck, pepper salted hair, moustache, brown hands clutching hers, slim hips and fancy, dusty boots.

Still barely dancing along, she pushed out of her boots one at a time and covered his silver snakeskin boots with her toes.

"You could get over Matthew Haines," her inner guide Mama said. Mama Duvall came into Jemmy's head whenever she wanted. Mama Duvall, Gabe's last, common-law wife. Mama had loved Jemmy best, and now she was dead.

Jemmy broke free from this Juan, gathered up her boots and pushed toward the door.

"Where you goin'?" the big waiter called across.

"Let her go," Juan said from behind. He came with her through the door.

"Still barely dancing along, she pushed out of her boots one at a time and covered his silver snakeskin boots with her toes."

She paused on the Jones Crossing mat, shoved her feet back in her boots.

She took her keys from her jeans pocket, found Matthew Haines' Bahmama condo number on a paper, and made her way across the truck stop lot. Juan crunched on behind her.

At her motel door she stopped, felt Juan's ghostly breath on her neck.

She turned around to face him. "What do you want with me?" she asked his green moon eyes in his shadow face.

He put a lean creased hand over hers. "I want to keep you from trouble, that's all."

She spun back, keyed her door and jumped in. The screen door slapped between them. "I got a phone call to make, have my guy to call."

"You don't have anyone to call," he said through the grey slotted light.

"I do," she said with tears. Anyway, Matthew Haines who'd used her like a mare, two years of mornings between Bambina and work, would want a call.

"Anybody you should call would be here with you now," Juan said. "Would not let you go up Idaho way all alone."

"Course, he couldn't be, Juan, I mean the man I call, he has obligations, he's busy and—"

"He don't answer the phone to you most of the time, little lady,"

"You're right...but only because he has Bambina and she's his obligation, taking his money and all and he—"

"Why don't you let me in here for a moment...Jemmy?"

She unlatched the screen.

Inside her room he pulled off his thick hunting jacket and folded it on a chair. He pushed Jemmima toward the bed edge. She sat right down, like beside Uncle Gabe on his porch those Idaho nights, long ago. Juan took her tanned hand in his own.

"There is only one obligation, little lady."

"What's that?" She looked down at their hands.

"Obligation is love, if it ain't here with you now, it ain't really true."

Tears filled her out. Juan sat there and held onto her until her eyes poured all they could. Then he rose and took up his shirt. She came with him to the door.

"Aren't you gonna ask me how—"he asked, once he was back gravel and spun 'round on truck light white rocks.

She smiled.

He smiled too.

"I could," she said, "but I already knew—my dead Mama sent you."

IVÁN SALINAS
VIGILIA

poetry readings are like church
because poetry is prayer

& poetry reminds me of mamá pera

I can invoke God in a poem and kill him in the same breath

Sitting here worshipping the poet
I listen to la palabra
I give my diezmo and support the space
because this is a temple
& read my books like catecismo
through the walls and out the streets
spread the word, hermanes
prediquen, your truth, the detail
of this moment on fire
the union of the stars
whatever heals your spirit

Metaphors be with you.

Poetry reminds me there is a prayer
to say every night
a poem that breaks bread
gets you on your knees
because you sin
but poetry doesn't ask you to forgive.

Poetry wants only what you can offer with your soul.
She wants your voice and no one else's
and its something kept between you and them
In the end there's no need to come to church
but don't expect a miracle in return

Come and worship all
your false idols
Come and become
a disciple

wheel up to the mic!

Come and get your communion!

¡Canta!
¡habla en lenguas!

Bless us! oh I beg you!

Muse, I love
how you pray
La santa palabra
maldita de mi alma
no me desampares
ni de dia ni de noche.

ELENA SECOTA   IT IS ALWAYS EVENING

She's a scene!
I could read my mother's impatient face
on the other side of customs
as I wait for my American passport to be stamped

1984
Bucharest airport feels like Alcatraz prison
after living as free as a monarch butterfly in London
and Los Angeles

I can tell the customs officer is secret police
They all are; short military style hair
intimidating stare
eying me to see if I crack

I am not about to let any doubt cross my face
I smile
the entry stamp is placed
I go through the barren doorway
to baggage claim

Did they open my suitcase?
Did they ransack my belongings
like the last time when the combination lock was pried open?
It is always evening…
Miraculously my suitcase is intact

Mother and Aunt Stella
stretched necks, waiting
There she is!
tears of joy run down our cheeks

Finally, we are in a taxi
silent
not a peep
it is widely known that most taxi drivers
are securitate - secret police informers

We step out into a darkness of austerity
to pay the country's debt
Not a street light in sight
only the occasional car zooming by

My suitcase is not only heavy but awkward like a blushing nun
Darling, my mother starts,
I dream of you arriving like the Queen of England carrying only a handbag
My mother is so right
that would be my dream, too
but how can one arrive from the West without gifts
for relatives behind the Iron Curtain
Aunt Stela finds a pole
threads it through the handle
we carry the gigantic suitcase stepping in and out of puddles

It is always night
when I visit my folks in communist Romania
eerie darkness
dogs bark all around
soon we will be home

Elena Secota, 2021

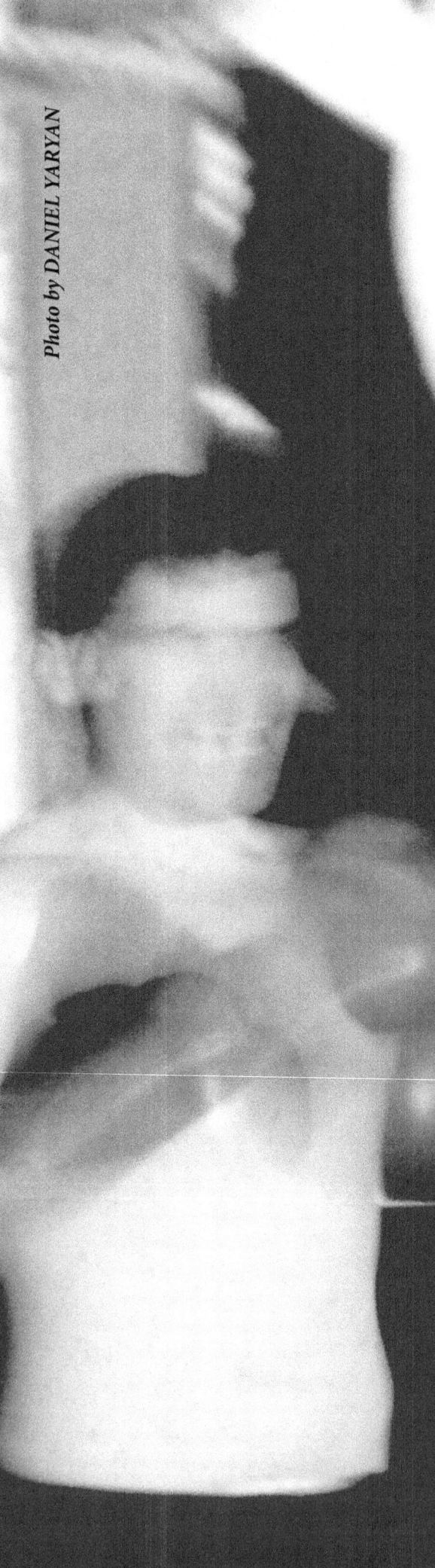

Photo by DANIEL YARYAN

MATT SEDILLO
TINEMIZ WAS HERE

First up
Shadowbox
 To break the dawn
Step jab
 Step back
Feint right
Check left
Hold the phone
Get low
Now dig to the body
 Dig to the body
 Dig to the body
Moves in silence
Jogs in place
In a house of four
Fast asleep
And slow to wake
In broken sweat
Palms his head
 Freshly cut
Freshly done
Fresh from
The demands of each new day
Reaching for the next
Reaches for the machete
Reaches for the hatchet
Just for the backyard
Just for the cactus
Man of the house
Ever since the accident
 In a small town
Where everybody knew
That boy had hands
Throws breakfast on the counter
And cans and a blackbook on his back
And the sky has not yet fallen
And the mountains
The color of deep ocean
And the wind carries
All the dreams
 Of this place
That the light of day has broken
 And it's red dirt roads are his
And it's gray cracked forks are his
And the side streets the back alleys
And all that there is here of heaven
Belongs to him
 And if he could
 He would take all that burns in this book
Pages of Nautl

Sketches of Calo
 Older than his years
Bigger than his time
 And bomb the sky
Of this town
 This house
This life
That grows
Smaller by the day
Returns home
To the smell of fresh nopales
And a hot plate
To his name around a table set
To the averted eyes
Of his pregnant girlfriend
To his sister
Wheeling in on cracked linoleum
To his mother's lament
About a government check
That doesn't quite stretch
The way that it used to
To her clasped hands
Of undying gratitude
To the good lord above
For having sent the extra income
Of a good son
Who turned out to be a good man
Just like his father before him
And the sun has risen
Morning has broken
 Pack it in kid
The day has now begun
And it's round two
Round two hundred miles
To Los Angeles
Where his uncle
Currently lives
Same man
Who taught the kid
To slip a jab
To rack a can
 That rivals don't rest
That nothing was handed
That any mark left
Would have to be taken
Same man
Who once taken away
Entrusted a name
Because he could not stop
Or outbox
 The demons within
And sometimes
 Yes sometimes

CONTINUED NEXT PAGE

When the kid closes his eyes
He can see him
In the distance
His uncle
Tio
Tocayo
Out in an ocean of mountain
Shadowboxing the night
And in that
Mystic act
They are one in the same
 And in his fists
Live
Myth
Legend
Tradition
The ancient
The sacred
 And if he could
 He would take all that burns in him
And carve
 Our legacy
Our lineage to the stars
So no one who came after us
Could ever mark us out
Or deny we were here
Throws an extra bag
A change of plans in the back
Could be a one way trip tells no one
Eyes peeled
 Hands on the wheel
In the driver's seat
Thinking long and deep
He recognizes the writers
On the trains
And he begins to dream
And when he dreams
 He is praying
And when he prays
He is dreaming
 Running and screaming
And the red dirt road Is sinking
Dear father
Who art dead and buried
Does anyone
Anywhere
Ever survive anything
Or are we all just passengers
To the end
Prisoners of guilt
Circumstance
And regret
Old man

How easy it must have been
 To have died young
 Before you could fuck it all up
Let them down
Walk on out
See how far your hands could carry you
And by the time
 They reach Los Angeles
Twin Towers
Correctional facilities
Where his uncle
Currently hangs his head
No explanation is expected or given
 The prison is on lockdown
Guests are to be turned away
They will leave
 He will stay
Spend the rest of the day
 Out in front of that towering dungeon
Hoping against the odds
His uncle will catch a glimpse of him
Shadowboxing the dusk
Step jab
Step back
Feint right
Check left
Bob and weave
Cut the ring
Now dig to the body
Dig to the body
Dig to the body
Now dig to the body
Dig to the body
That night he will seek out a trainyard
Fall to his knees
Close his eyes
 And begin to dream
Of his mother
His sister
His lady
The child she is carrying
Of the story
He will one day become
Should he choose to run
And he will see
For the first time
He has spent
His whole life
Chasing fathers
Figures and shadows
That were never
There to begin with
At least not

The way we cast them
But none of that matters now
See we are myth
We are legend
And it is now up to him
To reach into this bag
And do right
With what he has been
Entrusted
That night he will sleep
In the park
Next day
Board a bus
Return to the family
He so deeply loves
And these trains will leave their station
 Some ocean to ocean
 Carrying the name
He was given
Tinemiz
Meaning you will travel
You will live
And the starlit skies are his
And the open planes
The cityscapes
The uptowns
The downtowns
The small towns
That live in canyons
The backs of yards
And the hillside villages
The east sides
The south sides
The west sides
The north sides
The roaring metropolises
 And all there is of heaven
Belongs to him
And anyone anywhere
Across this land
Where trains cross tracks
Could see
 That boy had style
That boy had hands

Art by TRACY WITT

ALENE SMITH
LOST ON EARTH

As if to being - - lost creatures
from another planet
as to being sent here
an unknown purpose.
manifestations for all –
everything wrong on Earth – Hell…
Examples, samples of
madness, unraveled minds,
searching, searching…
for survival within
unknown destiny
scattered, hungry,
wondering, wandering, worry, weary, wistful - -
walking, walking, hiding, cringing, cowering
wanting from broken hearts, broken families,
broken focus, broken dreams, broken lives…
walking, walking, walking - - into oblivion…
we call them - - homeless.

November, 2021

EMI MOTOKAWA SONKSEN

EMI MOTOKAWA SONKSEN'S creations are inspired by spiritualism. She likes to take universal Buddhist concepts and interpret it through her modern, figurative style. Many of the characters she paints have big eyes because the eyes are the window to the soul. She hopes her creations will tickle your soul.

Emi was born in Tokyo, Japan and moved to Los Angeles at the age of seven. In 1995, she attended a Buddhist seminary in Tokyo and it was then when she first desired to translate Buddhist ideas into images. She has also crocheted several 3-foot Kokeshi dolls that were featured at the Japanese American Nation Museum. Emi's work is on Metro's "Through the Eyes of the Artist" poster series for the City of Monterey Park. It may be seen inside the Metro rail and buses running throughout L.A. County.

JEANNE MARIE SPICUZZA
THE AIR BETWEEN

There was a dream once
I leaned in to kiss you
and stopped at the air between

I sensed a breath
bereft of weeping
that caused me to pause

The thought that before
was just as important
as its momentary elimination

A precious prelude
to an untamed taste
precisely as vital as it feels

I sought to remember
my arid lips then
to a much greater appreciation

The acquaintance with yours
would make forever changed
the consorting molecules transformed

and through the two of us
I will miss the innocence
of an unquenched memory

yet welcome with anticipation
the movements embedded
in our vast, expansive communion

I cannot make perfect
this mission, but will commit
waking to its presence and execution

"El Viento" linoleum block print (4x9) by MELISSA WEST.

"Freeway Marathon" photo by S.A. GRIFFIN

MIKE SONKSEN
RUNNING AROUND THE CITY

My autobiography laced with poetry
accelerated at 18 running around the city
UCLA sociology understanding urban
Planning jumping geography creative
nonfiction flipping spoken word diction
backpack rap underground hip hop
garage band punk rock new left review
Kerouac blues Bukowski coffeehouse crews
open mic news choose your own adventure
enter the stage from the page wordplay
for days reading everyday about ancestors
an ongoing oral history always listening
keeping my ear around sacred ground
every part of town I could be found

By the late 90s I wanted to write professionally
but I wasn't quite sure how or where to do it
so I started hitting open mics anywhere I could
while in the daytime giving city tours & freelance
writing about neighborhoods & local music
every year I was moving from 18 to 30
Westwood, Sawtelle, Culver City, Hollywood,
Pico, Koreatown, Inglewood, Monterey Park
friendships the heart expansion & art
finding peace in public space & architecture
wishing the weather a window of inner work
I did an internet search for self worth
I found it on my shirt written in my heart
running around the city kickstarted the art

CARL STILLWELL (aka CaLokie)
MANA [2]

Mana is
Bahaman Brahmans chanting mantras before a Madagascar dawn,
high noon profits of a Mama & Papa pot shop in Chicago,
jogging off millions of Machiavellian manipulations on Saginaw sidewalk,
the magic of a margarita with a Mohammedan Madonna in March

               Mana is SUNRISE
           Mana is DAYTIME
Mana is SUNSET
Mana is NIGHTTIME
Mana is
spring cantatas of rocking Rachmaninof' and be-bopping Bach,
Jimi Hendrix, Joe Cocker, Santana and Janis Joplin at Woodstock,
manioc madness manifested at a Madison, Wisconsin stomp dance,
a Sasquatch munching Choctaw chocolate on a frozen Mackinaw swamp
               Mana is spring INFANCY
           Mana is summer ADOLESCENCE
Mana is autumn MATURITY
Mana is winter wisdom of ELDERS
Mana is
the Taj Mahal love of Shah Jahal for his wife, Mumtaz,
the prophetic poetry of a pentecostal Hobbit in Managua mañana,
applauding Amada Delgado's Tecate Tocatta at Montana cocktail lounge,
the colossal saxophone of Sonny Rollins melting Stockholm frost
               As far as East
           is from West
and North from
South is MANA
Mana is
the cosmic immensity of a Ma Yüan monochromatic ink drawing,
Dietrich Bonhoeffer detoxification of Nazi demagoguery,
Mayahana contacts with Yahweh through Allen Watts radio talks,
the Pascal thought we're nothing before the ALL but ALL toward the nothing
               Mana is BEYOND
           Mana is WITHIN
Mana is the beyond within
Ommmmmmmmmmmmmmmmmmmmmmmmmmmmmmmmmmmmmmm

—CaLokie

[2]*The Polynesian, Melanesian, and Maori belief
in a pervasive supernatural or magical power*

S.B. Stokes at Poetry Festival Santa Cruz, 2/12/12. Photo by ELLA SENERES.

S.B. STOKES
MCCLURE, MCFERRIN, AND ABOUT
A HUNDRED OTHER PEOPLE SINGING..

does touching hands
count for anything
like a whispered promise
when you close your eyes

thinking your singing voice
will eventually lead you back
toward the shimmering direction
of animals
whose shapes defy simple explanation

can you wind back a moment
or recall a dream
you've had over 23 times
both while awake and while
in that other torturous state

thinking that opening your lips wide
but not making any sound
could be the same as kissing

the chapped back of your own
lonely hand

squinting at yourself
in a cracked mirror
giving the same familiar feeling
as a melody wafting
from an undefined direction
on the salted wind
of a white tipped bay

will your wishes ever
become a song
sung in smiling harmony
with the still unknown
still undefined
love of your
achingly meager life

if you sing it
could your reedy desires
become enough
to push your tired and wilting body
through a mathematically perfect song?

"Horse Conjuring a Man" etching by DON LA VIERE TURNER (1960).

KEVIN PATRICK SULLIVAN
Horse Conjuring A Man
from an Etching by
Don La Viere Turner

She knew her breath had to be hot
She remembered an angel
Without wings
She wanted this touch
This connection outside herself
She wanted to be ridden
Feel those legs against her sides
That stroke on her long face

She had no idea

        He would make
Spurs and whips

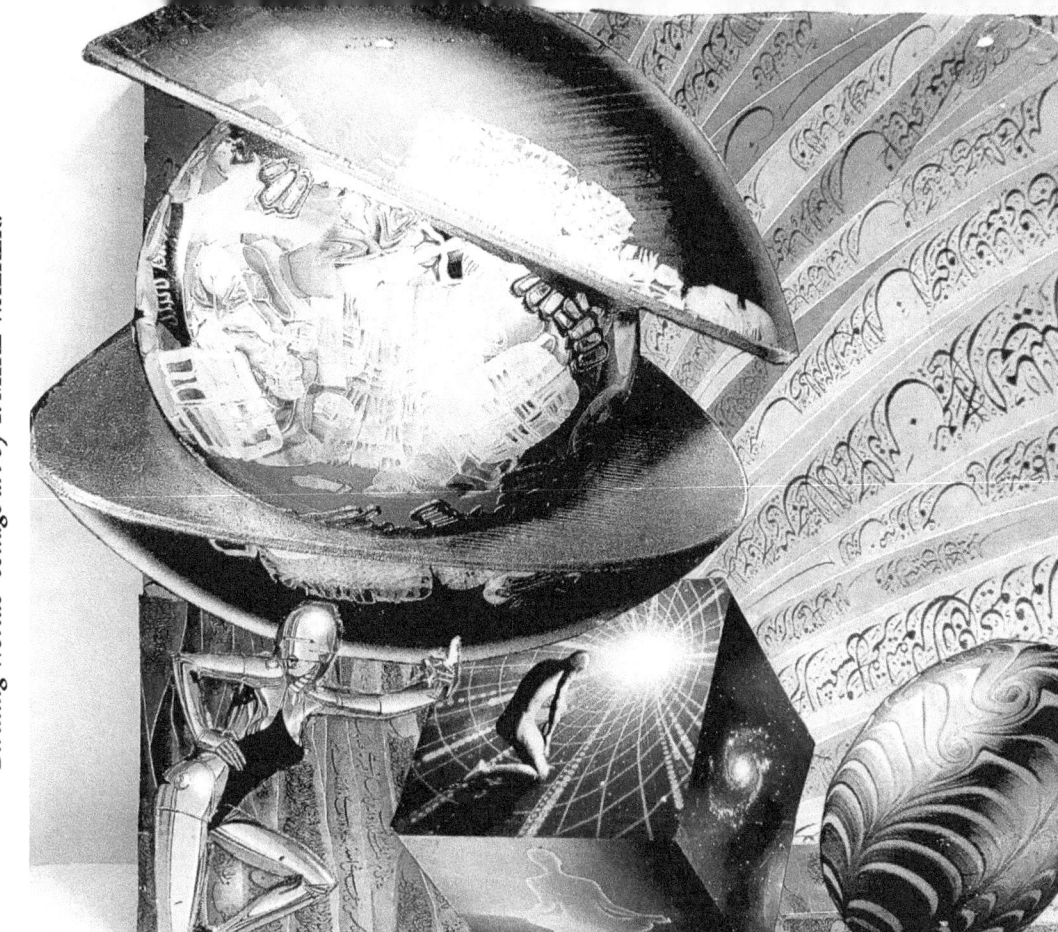

"Birthing Worlds" collage art by T. MIKE WALKER.

KEVIN PARTICK SULLIVAN
ROBOT LOVE

I think of Data from Star Trek: The Next Generation
Of R2D2 and C3PO from Star Wars
Of the robot Robbie from Lost in Space
But I'm going all the way back to the Tin Man
From the Wizard of Oz – if I only had a heart
So there he was teaming up with a Scare Crow – a brain
A young woman with a dog – I want to go home –I just want to go home
And a cowardly lion – courage yea that's all I need – courage
Notice I said teaming up because for me that is important
We cannot get there from here alone
There is something big as the sky inside you
A blue cloudless sky
An ocean
Inside you are the dreams I look for in my waking
I need your heart – your mind – your courage
If I'm ever to get home where all my life is sweet
Childlike and we are hitting our stride
You and me – all of us together
And maybe some love
Not robot love
But real love–
Yea!
A real human love
One love
One planet
A blue cloudless sky inside you!
Yea!!!
An ocean inside you!

MANI SURI
MEANING OF LIFE

I saw moss clinging to a barren rock on Palma Majorca, many moons ago.
I didn't hear it ask why or what for.
I thought of a peacock strutting in a garden.
It didn't ask either.
Nor does a gazelle leaping across the Serengeti.
The chimp swinging from branch to branch didn't stop mid-lurch to ask either.
Not even a whisper of any such query from the prey gasping for air, caught in its predator's fangs
and claws.
Then why do I,
with the gift of human intellect and fruit basket of civilization,
set aside living,
only to ponder questions to which
there are no answers?

Breathe, live, help others do the same.

Create beauty, comfort, share with humanity to help it cherish life
not despair.

One step.
Next step.
Two step.
Dance.
Rejoice!

The Sun still rises after the storm.

Cliché suivant.

Collage art by T. MIKE WALKER.

Art by LYNN ROGERS.

PJ SWIFT
WAITING IN LINE

Waiting in line at the post office to pick up my package, I saw him. Wearing his dark Lennon shades low on his nose, he had the same droopy eyelids with that bright, joyous twinkle in his eyes. His cap sat on his head at a smooth angle, as his baggy pants hung comfortably on his slim frame, and his feet lazily filled his slippers just partway. Across the hall from me, S.P. stood calm and relaxed. His long delicate fingers caressed his envelope as if composing a tune. Just like the S.P. I knew. But this man appeared East Asian. And S.P., a pale redhead, was not. And there was also the fact that S.P. had been dead for over half a year.

Yet this man was surely him. His manner, nature, and essence were all S.P. I studied him from a distance, unsure if he registered my gaze. Delivering his envelope ahead of me, he appeared to flash a wry smile for my benefit before raising his shades and sauntering away.

I clumsily held my large package, shifting it from arm to arm as I stared at where he had just stood.

I had heard of such people before. But only now had I been aware of encountering one. This man was more than a doppelganger. This man must have been an immortal vessel -- an animated body available to accept the transient souls of the dead. Just as he must have been doing continually since time eternal, temporarily hosting an expedited reincarnation.

Of course, S.P. must have encountered such a fate. He shared so much joy and connection with our current world. Why should he wait to be reborn and grow into a new age when his soul needed to engage with the here and now? Ours was the age he knew best, one that he also helped form through his sensitive charm and rebellious but enlightened manner.

This man, this host of S.P., possessed a coolness and reserve that allowed him to be present while just out of sight. He had the know-how to wander through this world with his light touch of grace and, every now and then, to deliver a wink and a smile to let people know that their friends were okay.

Art by
CHARLES BUKOWSKI
from the Kamstra
Sparchive Collection.

WILLIAM TAYLOR, JR.
LIKE BUKOWSKI'S SHOELACE

The great loneliness of the world
like some perfect eternal machine

I pace its belly
as the hours fall away

this moment to moment
makes me nervous

this milling about until the Next
Terrible Thing

the ceaseless trickling
of ordinary dooms

wearing us down like
Bukowski's shoelace

and we're expected to hold it all
together long enough to die

in rebuttal I drink beer
and watch the people walk

along Polk Street beneath
the August sun

they talk and laugh
as if there were still

a chance for something

and I cling to it like
my last ticket home.

WILLIAM TAYLOR, JR.
SHAKING IT OFF

Friends, let's celebrate
this moment simply because it's here
and will never be so again.

They're playing the Velvet Underground
at Mr. Bing's in Chinatown

it's a sunny afternoon in April
and death wouldn't dare

show its face on such a day,
not around here.

Sure, the dark got ahold of me early on

but I can still shake it off a bit

with another stupid poem
another golden beer beneath
a golden sun.

Let the love and the light
slip through the cracks
as they will.

Let me have this

as the people drink
and laugh and smoke

as the old love songs play
and play like nothing
could ever end.

Photo of Pamela Twining and Andy Clausen (2015) by MARCIA WARD.

Sparring Legacies
FOOTSTEPS
OF THE **WIND**

PAMELA TWINING
November 27, 1950 – Saturday, July 8, 2023

Pamela Kathryn Twining lived in Woodstock, NY, where she raised her children and studied organic farming and healing with herbs. She read her poetry in many venues, alongside her partner Andy Clausen, Peter Lamborn Wilson, Mikhail Horowitz, Anne Waldman, Antler, Jeff Poniewaz, and Charles Plymell, to name a few, often accompanied by Cosmic Legends. Over the years she developed a very personal style, sometimes tender and lyrical, sometimes brutally frank, resonating with the wisdom of her partially Native American heritage. An area resident since 1972, she attended Vassar College in Poughkeepsie. Pamela was New York State Beat Poet Laureate 2022-2024.

Twining's work has appeared in *Big Scream, Napalm Health Spa, The Café Review, Big Hammer, Sparring With Beatnik Ghosts Omnibus, Poetrybay* and others. Pamela is the author of *i have been a river…; Selected Poems of Pamela Twining* (DancinFool Press 2011), *utopians & madmen* (DancinFool Press 2012) and *A Thousand Years of Wanting: The Erotic Poetry of Pamela Twining* (Shivastan Press 2013).

Twining died Saturday, July 8, 2023 at the Health Alliance Hospital, Mary's Ave. Campus, Kingston, New York. She was born November 27, 1950 in Silver Spring, MD. She was the daughter of the late Perry Ford Twining and Constance Cole Twining. Her survivors include her partner, Andy Clausen; three daughters: Morgan (Dean) Sasser of GA., Charlotte Nelson of Kingston and Raven Twining of Fla.; a son, Erich Ploutz of West Hurley. Two brothers: Dana and Terry Twining and six grandchildren: Kane Twining, Colden Staccio, Shawn Quick, Pablo Villar-Nelson, Annabelle and Jasmine Ploutz. Several nieces and nephews also survive.

PAMELA TWINING
SOLITAIRE

I

O jack how long since
unending questions
the spunglass poets who had the knack
of this modern lingo
the free flowing worded wordless cacophony
of life in this time
broken bent twisted
living with desires and understandings on their sleeves
burgeoning bloody electricity of information
never known in light of bombs
dropped from the sky
populations annihilated, their faces unseen

jack if you were alive now what would you say?
would you abandon poetry in disgust?
turn from speaking Truth because no one's listening?
descend into crotchety old man complaints of "kids today"?
you were the ego to Cassady's id, and Allen was superego
if Ray was the Buddha, Gregory was Loki Trickster

the joy of being unRealized
a Youthquake cohort massive swelling
in the digestive tract of the race of humankind
moving along we're moving along to be excreted into the Void
as all tips backwards to an even less enlightened time
instilling fear of starvation in a world of plenty
fear of forcible submission in a world of unprecedented freedom
fear of Otherness in a world of overwhelming Oneness
no reason for unBrothering

so many things have changed
since you and your companions sought the jazz streets
back night alleys sweet whiskey, smoke and untamed minds
unfettered words still shocking enough to Break the Glass!
tear holes in the envelope of time
since you om'd in the limitless starry night
alone with the mountaintop ghosts
of adventures yet to come

an early leaver, you never saw what you had wrought
a generation released upon the roads
the Joy of Seeking burning youthful eyes

who can know what distortions, what manipulative ploys
of those who control the purse strings
who let us live by their grace and call it God?

*Collage art
by T. MIKE
WALKER.*

Sparring Legacies
FOOTSTEPS
OF THE **WIND**

Look into the faces of imprisoned men released
from life sentences based on lies
creeping up out of the darkness of no family
no loving touch
no work in the world
their faces so pale and grateful
writhing in the embraces of those denied too long
the evidence there all along
suppressed unknown and unacted upon
as their youthful dreams and nightmares withered dead
like scorched leaves in the holocaust of racism
trapped in cells where turning around, where stretching out
was seen as sweet liberty
all that could be dreamed of
under the malicious engineering of a system
where the least-haves are forced to accept responsibility
for the ills of a society lost to consciousness

we are lost we are lost
children grown old taking care of their families
in the exploding streets
still playing in the rubble as the sun sets again
on the torn apart memories of innocence and awe
blasted away with the limbs of their best friends gunned down in the road
sliced open by shards flying before the hot breath of bombs
once dewy complexions blasted with holes
lying in spreading dark pools of the essence
that made them the bright sparks of breath
the golden lights of longing
the ones we love

the cock crows thrice
and rosy dawn creeps out again across the shattered lands
a solitary wanderer joins with all the gone voices
open ears open skies
listening to the silence of the grave
the soft susurration of the rain
the infinite birth pains of leaf and bud
the sounds of children playing
the sounds of children playing

"Creation" linoleum block print by MELISSA WEST.

"SR29 Napa"
linoleum block
print by
MELISSA WEST.

"Kerouac" painting by MARC OLMSTED.

CHRIS VANNOY
LAST CALL FOR KEROUAC

his elbows would have rested just so
spread wide across the wood bar rail
polished with the sweat of hard worked men
with tired eyes

he would have watched
silently
as the foam slid to the bottom of the glass
now empty in his hand
remembering Johnny Carson and his mother, always his mother
always,
his mother

I see him
drained
sheltering from the baking sun
and from the humidity that seals his shirt to his skin
raising his head each time the door creaks
wondering if the blood that he coughed up this morning
would be his last
or if another wasted day
would follow this downward spiral
as he gradually slips
into a familiar madness
numbed
as the liquid-cool drains through him

then, after his stumble home,
just before the dark of sleep takes him in its kindness
he would remember another road
that began with Ginsberg and Burroughs
and ended with Neal
dead on the tracks in Mexico.

MERRITT WALDON
DREAM ABOUT BRAUTIGAN

a dream once drilled in to my wet grey
mind

it was of Richard Brautigan violently screaming
in some kind of thick void

as i drew closer with a lamp

there he was
violently beating &
cursing a bright yellow
typewriter

its bits cried out to
this pumping heart

all of a sudden it was very quiet

he was sitting in a blue velvet chair weeping

"why do you make me hate you so?"
he yelled at the machine

as i awoke in the haze between sleep
& waking

i could see his phantom

drinking a cup of instant coffee

writing secret dreams for a lost
hitch-hiker

"Ghost Dwelling" background art by TRACY WITT.

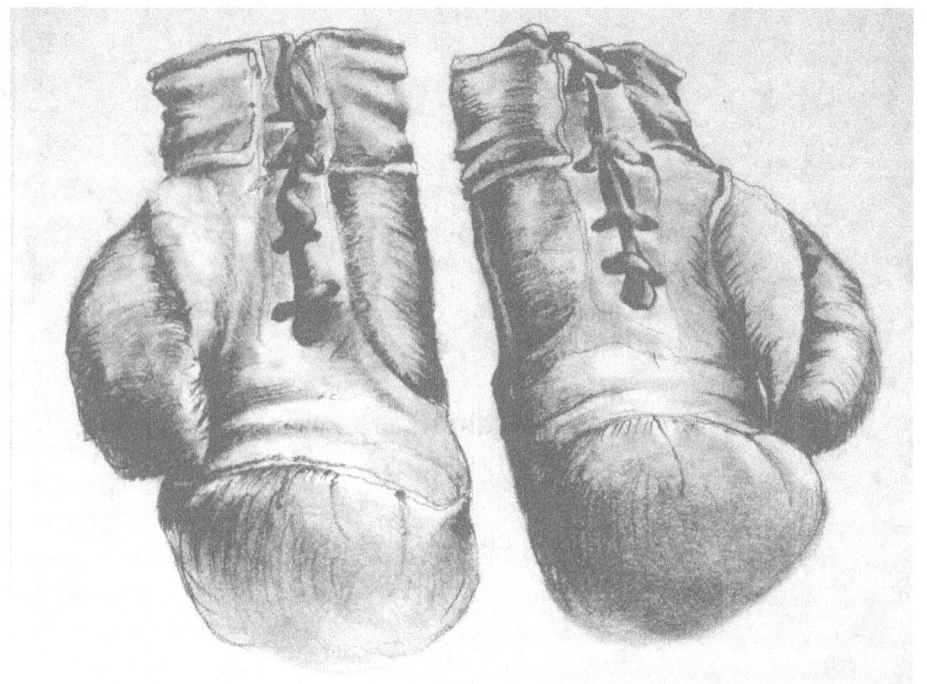

Art by TRACY WITT.

T. MIKE WALKER
SHORT PUNCHES

THE STORM

The Storm took out the tree
But I took out the storm in me
And walked it by the raging sea
And danced upon the sand until
We both were free...The storm, and me.

NIGHT

Blessed are the sleepless
For they shall inherit the night;
The blossoms of stars,
The Moon's fickle light;
Labyrinths of waking dreams
That make us laugh and yawn
And cringe from dark terrors
Dispelled by the dawn.

A MARRIAGE NOT

So we will go our separate ways
And sing our separate songs,
So each of us can do our 'right'
Without the other's 'wrong'

RECIPROCITY

You breath out what I breath in
So don't pollute the air, my friend,
You breath in what I breath out
That's what sharing's all about.
You have needs that you want met
And I have needs, so don't forget
That what you give is what you get.

SPIRITUAL SEX

On a slick silver scooter all dressed in white robes
She swept through the town like a transparent ghost

From lover to lover from stranger to friend,
She wrapped them in love from beginning to end

What was her motive, what were her views?
She brought to each lover the beautiful news

That each one was worthy of ungrudging love
That Spiritual Sex was a Gift from Above

That you've got it today, but tomorrow its gone,
That no matter how good, it won't last for long

She delivers her news with a kiss, then departs,
Soothing their loins, while stealing their hearts.

IT'D NICE TO SEE DOGS OUT WALKING THEIR PEOPLE
Who follow obedient, poop bags in hand,
Tied to their leashes or romping in parks,
Chasing their Frisbee's and balls,
Interspecies Communication,
Nation of Dog-People making connections
By sniffing each other out.
Woof & Growl & Bark

GEORGE WALLACE
MANIFESTO SONG

This is a song to be sung poorly
For a man with no work
For a school with no books
For a woman with no roof top
A song for a musician whose guitar has been ripped out of his hands
A song without a guitar to sing it with
A song
   sung
      poorly
To scold god for giving us a land with not enough love in it

This is a song to be sung poorly
To raise Hell
To punish Heaven
To break bread with the damned
To be sung poorly because it is impossible to raise a child with dignity in a land like this
      How long, how long, can this go on
  (This is my heart
    This is my country
  As if god cares)
Sing this song poorly
It is our manifesto

Photo by DANIEL YARYAN

PAM WARD
EXHAUST

She detested it.
Right down to the
ride up there.
Counting Denny's
signs and cars
broke down.
The fake Aztec
look of the suburbs.
It reminded her
of thin
see-through
curtains
chipped
rotten tile
that smoky
dead smell
of motel rooms.
And why
she left him
for good
she thought
that time
all the busted
up plates
stacks of
ripped pictures
her good dresses
shoved in
the trash can.
How he called
her again
and again
'til she finally
picked up
his voice
in one smog
oozing plea.
And the only
thing worse
the only thing
worse than
that dry
separation
was being
with him now
on this hot
vinyl seat
on another
long ride to
his mother's.

SCOTT WANNBERG
FEB. 20, 1953 – AUG.19, 2011

Sparring Legacies
FOOTSTEPS
OF THE **WIND**

SCOTT WANNBERG
THE NOISES WE MAKE ON THE HEADS OF OUR PINS

The noises we make
when thunder dances on the head of a pin.
The entire package of our lives
ready for delivery along a road
that takes too many prisoners.

There are sound systems that light up in
the hard to sustain dark.
They name our handicraft and
there is no limit to the number of instruments
that get out of jail to be played
in the true moment.

Call collect and the voice of
ongoing love will be delivered to your door,
with no questions asked.

We dance as best as the legs will go.

We dance and nobody hands us a ticket.

Scott Wannberg
4/23/2005

Opposite page: Collage art by T. MIKE WALKER.

"Dawn Runners" ollage art by T. MIKE WALKER.

DIG WAYNE
SOUND CLUSTER

drop your leaded forearms indweller of sym-phony

leave yourself susceptible to a divine influence

this stagnant debris flow is crucifying horns and flowers

put a window in the strings so the octaves can escape if need be

let the hungry bassoons fend for themselves for once

dip the French horns in fondue while they're still warm

inform the bullied piccolos the coast is clear - the tympani mallets have been reported

ridicule aimed at the triangle will be dealt with silently

calling the maestro, dude will no longer be tolerated after 6PM

embracing this morass of illegal harmonics is the next big existential fuegazie

gird your lonely cello loins gather your 44-piece parure of sound trinkets,
let them walk through walls of enlightenment,
improvise new lies that become cosmic truths that bring us closer
to expansion beyond knowledge,
to a sound we've only tasted, seen, felt smelled, smelly smelled
but never heard or we may not return to the air under our souls,
scary souls, bleeding as we yearn to fly comfortable with mystery,
searching for the grace wave of, I dare you

RUTH WEISS
JUNE 24, 1928 – JULY 31, 2020

ruth weiss by ANN COHEN.

ruth weiss
for WANDA COLEMAN
11/13/1946 – 11/22/2013

couldn't stop the blood-clots
like haiku to the point
exclamation marks
morse code
signals for your departure heeded
gathering enough strength
to belt out your message
again & again

THE SPIRIT LIVES ON
NO STOPPERS POSSIBLE

you paid with your blood of the poet

ruth weiss
march 2014

A.D. WINANS
POEM FOR RUTH WEISS

she shadowboxes with father time
daytime nighttime bebop jazz time
she dances with timeless time
all rhythm no rhyme

birds in flight flap their wings
copulate with the wind
feed off the flesh of the other
in roller coaster freeze-stop motion

she sings her song daytime nighttime
bitch slaps father time
Kaufman son of jazz in her heart
Micheline in her blood

jazz in the Fillmore
jazz on Harlem rooftops
full moon rising
with poems that dig into my bones
lubricate the gears of my mind
lost in a haze of motionless motion

A.D. WINANS
THE SONG OF LIFE

an unseen band plays to the audience
or is it just inside my head
I peer out at those gathered to hear me read
a row of books peers from the nearby bookshelf
wants to sing to the young woman in jeans
and a flower in her hair
a sea of warm faces sits attentively
in folding chairs

a young man in a black beret and turtleneck
relives the Beatnik era
Annie with her warm smile
my friend Paul in the front row
Neeli takes notes in his red notebook

a sweet melody plays inside my head
lingers there with poet friends long dead
the beat of the heart a crazed drummer
beats inside my chest

a small child breaks free from her mother
wants the feel of a book
but she can only reach the bottom shelf
left perhaps with dreams of what is and might be

the reading begins
the present the past flirt with the future
I sprinkle in a bit of laughter
mates to darkness empathy and compassion
ingredients for a soul cake
connect with the audience
swim out to sea like Gene Ruggles book
"Lifeguard in the Snow."

warmed by the smiles in the audience
I shed ancestral baggage
emerge in the light of speech
the song of life sings in my bones

A.D. Winans photo by HANNAH YARYAN.

A.D. WINANS
REMEMBERING BOB KAUFMAN

He walked the streets of North Beach
An ancient warrior with hollow eyes
His eyes bore into you like a drill
Forced to carry decades of heavy sorrow
On his back like a bent-over hunchback
Overcome with the rust of time
Flesh stripped to the marrow
The mirror of his eyes did a slow dance
Up and down Grant Avenue
A dark shadow riding clouds of "Ancient Rain"
His life measured in hot jazz and verse
A surreal mirage where hip cats
Wailed in precision rhythm

He walked an imaginary zoo
Looking for tigers to talk too
Runaway poems blaring in his ears
Like a stuck car horn
The Ancient Rain falling
Falling
Falling
Washing away his wounds

A Trip to the Moon by GEORGES MÉLIÈS

DANIEL YARYAN
GEORGES MÉLIÈS POEM

a trip to the moon
Georges Méliès made it sooner
mind flight spectacle

effects wizard king
Méliès brought eyes everything
then left with nothing

filmmaker magic
illusions hold up past his fate
barouche bound for stars

may planets align
marvel his celestial hearth
feast on Méliès films

Apollo might hear
artists plight at tycoon hands
fire vengeance arrows

new immortal Méliès
brings artists favor to Gods
create in peace - yes!

WILLIAM EVERSON
THESE ARE THE RAVENS

These are the ravens of my soul,
Sloping above the lonely fields
And cawing, cawing.
I have released them now,
And sent them wavering down the sky,
Learning the slow witchery of the wind,
And crying on the farthest fences of the world.

Sparring Legacies
FOOTSTEPS
OF THE WIND

AFTERWORD:

Thanks to Special Feature Editor S.A. Griffin for his work curating the **Doug Knott** Tribute section and for bringing the poems of **Scott Wannberg** and **Frank T. Rios** to the readers of *Sparring Artists*!

Happy 45th year in Los Angeles, S.A.!

— *Daniel Yaryan*

Photo of S.A. Griffin by LORRAINE PERROTTA

TRADE PAPERBACKS NOW AVAILABLE!

HARDBOUND 8.5 X 11 DELUXE EDITIONS NOW AVAILABLE!

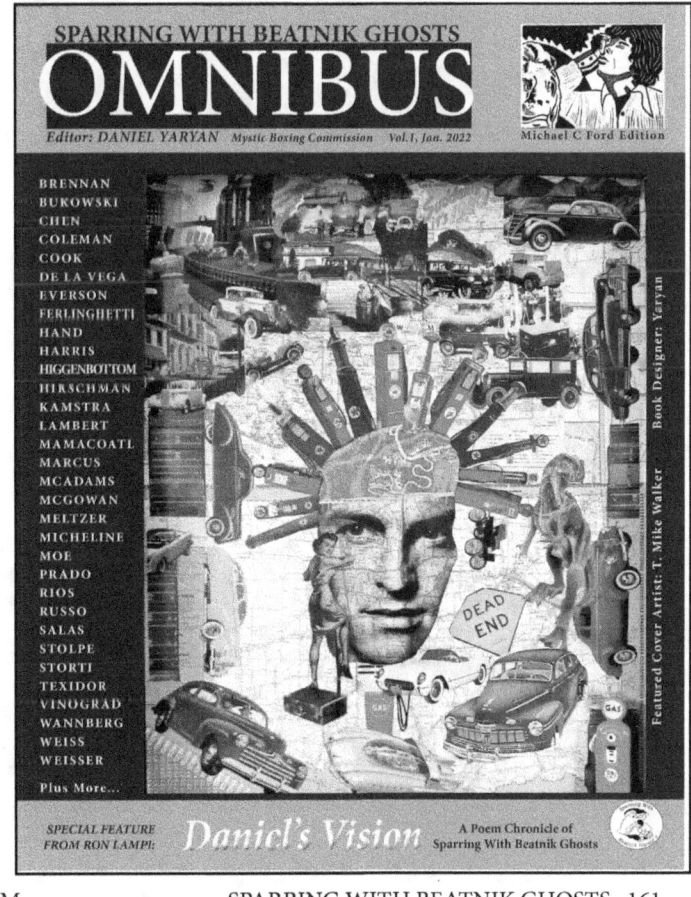